four secrets

four secrets

Margaret Willey

carolrhoda LAB
MINNEAPOLIS

Carolrhoda Lab™
An imprint of Carolrhoda Books
A division of Lerner Publishing Group, Inc.
241 First Avenue North
Minneapolis, MN 55401 U.S.A.

For updated reading levels and more information, look up this title at
www.lernerbooks.com.

Cover and interior images © iStockphoto.com/pixitive (crow silhouettes).

Main body text set in Janson Text 11/15.
Typeface provided by Linotype AG.

Library of Congress Cataloging-in-Publication Data

Willey, Margaret.
          Four secrets / by Margaret Willey.
               p.   cm.
          Summary: Through journal entries required by their social worker at a
     juvenile detention center, middle-schoolers Katie, Nate, and Renata relate
     how they came to kidnap their tormentor, Chase, a star athlete from the
     town's most prominent family.
          ISBN: 978–0–7613–8535–6 (trade hard cover : alk. paper)
          ISBN: 978–1–4677–0011–5 (eBook)
          1. Secrets—Fiction. 2. Best friends—Fiction. 3. Friendship—Fiction.
     4. Kidnapping—Fiction. 5. Bullies—Fiction. 6. Diaries—Fiction. 7. Juvenile
     detention homes—Fiction.] I. Title.
     PZ7.W65548Pac 2012
     [Fic]—dc23   2011044344

Manufactured in the United States of America
2 – SB – 12/31/13

Dedicated to the memory of Virginia L. Gordon,
first reader and beloved friend

The road must be trod, but it will be very hard. And neither strength nor wisdom will carry us far upon it. This quest may be attempted by the weak with as much hope as the strong. Yet such is oft the course of deeds that move the wheels of the world: small hands do them because they must, while the eyes of the great are elsewhere.

—Elrond, Elf-Lord,
The Lord of the Rings, J. R. R. Tolkien

First GreyMount Katie

The social worker is making me write in a journal, starting today. She said that I need to explain in my own words how it all began. She means the kidnapping. She said I should be completely honest because no one will see the journal except her and she won't let anyone use what I write against me. Her big thing is she really wants to help me and I believe her. She can't help me. But she wants to; that's her job.

It's my second day of juvie, Journal, and I'm in personal time, which is when you get to sit around after lunch and do an activity of your own choosing before afternoon classes start. Three of the other girls in Pod A (my pod) are reading books from the juvie library and one of them is reading *Christian Life Magazine* and one is in her room doing whatever and one other girl is sitting alone at a table in the Common Area, writing in a journal, same as me.

Okay, I need to focus, I only have half an hour. I need to go back in time and do the how-it-all-began thing, describe the day that everything changed and I turned into a criminal.

I'm stuck already, Journal! I'm stuck because I'm just not sure how it all began. When did it start? When did we change? There wasn't a day. There wasn't even a week. I never really thought about it this way before—an actual beginning to the mess we're in.

Okay, there was that one day back in April when the three of us first talked for real about finding a way to stop Chase Dobson from hurting Renata. It was after school and we were on our way to the Dairy Dog, and Nate was walking a little behind us. He was talking about honor and courage, and saying we had to stop thinking like slaves and we had to have a plan. Then he started making up a plan as he walked, describing it more like a fantasy, like one of his stories, or something that could only happen in a dream. And his plan was that we needed first of all to get Chase alone. Away from his friends. And while I was listening, it suddenly struck me that maybe Nate's plan didn't need to be a fantasy or a dream; maybe it could happen for real, if we all agreed to it and if we did it as a team. If we could get Chase alone, maybe we really could make him listen to us. I looked at Renata, and I swear she was having the very same thought. And then Nate stopped walking. And then Renata and I stopped walking. We turned around and looked at Nate, standing very still on the sidewalk. This LOOK passed between the three of us, and the look almost had a buzzing sound, it was so powerful and real. We sent the look back and forth between us a few more times, and then Nate said *yes*. That was all he said, he said—*yes*, softly but bravely. And then Renata said *yes*. And then I said *yes*. And then a loud YES! rose up from us and united us in our plan. We were united, Journal. We were going to take a stand. We were going to stop Chase. Was that the beginning of it?

Or was it the day in Renata's bedroom when she first told me what Chase was doing to her and she started to cry and I had never seen her cry before that? That was in April too. I watched her tears come all down her face, and it changed me. Those tears turned me to steel inside. That was when I became First GreyMount Katie, the girl who could do anything, including things that the old Katie would never have done, including the things that got me locked up in juvie, me who has never been in trouble with anybody but my mom. Were Renata's tears the beginning?

Or was it even farther back, all the way back to last year, to when Renata first appeared at our school? Was it the day this tiny girl walked up to us and asked us if she could *please* sit with us on the end of our cafeteria table and we didn't say anything at first because she had just the slightest southern accent and it sounded really cute and different and because she had said please in the first place and because she was wearing her brown-almost-black hair super short and standing kind of straight up at her forehead and it looked kind of goth but mostly amazing and because her eyes were HUGE and brown, brown, brown with dark eyebrows. She was perfect, Journal. And from that moment, she was completely, COMPLETELY, my best friend. The kind of friend you will do anything for. The kind of friend Nate already was.

She told us her name. And then she smiled, crinkling up those brown eyes. Okay, I'm deciding it right now—that was the beginning—that moment when one minute there was no Renata and the next minute there was a Renata, asking to be with us, wanting to sit down with us, the two losers, eating with our heads down in that awful cafeteria.

I have to stop. Lee Ann is asking for the pens to be turned in. I have to go to World History. I'll write more after Gym class.

Journal Entry June 8—After Gym

Why do I hate junior high? I need to explain. I've only ever gone to the public schools in North Holmes, so I don't know if all schools are like mine, but at North Holmes they have this thing that can happen in your social life, from out of the blue, and there is even a code word for it—it's called getting *stung*. It happens when your group of friends decides you're dragging the group down in popularity, and so the other people in your clique sting you. They become like scorpions; they sting you till you die. This is done in many ways involving Facebook, notes, texts, rumors, and whispers. It takes about a week. There does not have to be a reason. Everybody does their part—and presto. You are gone, Journal. You are just gone.

It happened to me at the beginning of eighth grade. When I told Mom, she said there was no use caring, since every single kid who had stung me was a disgrace to the human family.

Nate: She really said that? She called them a disgrace to the human family? God, I love your mom so much.

Me: Did you tell your mom?

Nate: I don't tell Sylvia anything. Talking to her would interrupt her schedule of prayer.

I don't know why our friends decided to sting us both at the same time, but it was even more excruciating, because we felt as bad for each other as we did for ourselves. We had become each other's best friend ever since last year, when we'd spent most of our weekends hanging out at my house. There are many reasons why Nate is my best friend—I couldn't begin to tell them all, but here are the two biggest: number one—he is the only boy I know who really cares about other people's feelings. He is just so nice; my mom says he is like a boy from another century. Reason number two—he is a genius. Secretly, privately, a genius writer—he writes amazing fantasy stories about knights and battles and kingdoms, and he has written at least three finished stories already, and they are so good that I know that someday he will be famous, and I might be famous too just for being his friend. Also I should mention he is super handsome, but I don't like him in that way.

Journal Entry June 8—Evening Personal Time

I decided I'm going to write about what we said to each other like it's a play. Not like I know anything about writing plays, but I am just really interested in how people talk to each other when they are upset or scared or angry or really, really happy. I am very, very interested in this. My mom always said that I have a good ear for knowing what people are trying to say, even when they aren't exactly saying it. Also I remember what people said like months ago, even when I have forgotten other details. Plus I really like how when you read a play, all you have are the characters' spoken words. Like those words are all that matter in the universe of the play. This is not at all like what Nate does when he writes. He includes all kinds of details and descriptions and puts everything in fantasy language, like from days of yore or whatever. Anyway, I was thinking that if I write our conversations like scenes in a play and not worry about every single detail, it might help me to remember. Especially the parts that are kind of awful to remember.

Like for example, the week after I got stung was a blur of terrible days, but I remember clearly that moment when my mom called my ex-friends a disgrace to the human family. And I asked her if she was including Nate.

Mom: Oh Honey, please don't tell me that Nate is one of the kids who did this mean thing to you.

Me: He didn't. He wouldn't. He's my best friend. The kids at school did the same thing to him.

Mom: Oh for Pete's sake, what did I tell you? Are you listening to me? I have never liked those spoiled kids you were hanging around with. And now look at them—persecuting the only genius in their midst!

She meant Nate, not me, Journal. She's crazy about Nate because he talks to her and laughs at her jokes. Mom used to think I was a genius. Before Renata came, before we started fighting all the time. In fact, when everything was over and we were on our way to the detention center to be what is called *arraigned*, we were fighting. Mom was manhandling me in the car outside the juvenile court building, holding my chin really tight and making me look her in the eye.

Mom: For the first time in your life you are in too much trouble to talk your way out of it, Miss Smarty-girl. Did you know that? Did you know that, Miss Super Brain?

*Me: Maybe I'm not such a Super Brain, okay? Maybe I
made a mistake, okay? Maybe you made a mistake!
God, Mom! Just deal with it!*

I was trying to jerk my head away from her terrible grip. She kept squeezing my chin, making me look in her eyes. I closed my eyes tight, hating her. Sometimes I do kind of hate her, Journal. Her breath was all up in my face. Her voice was a raspy whisper.

Mom: Why are you doing this to me, Katie?

Seriously, she thinks everything I do is about her.

She was the one who always told me that you shouldn't take it when people try to mess with you. People are supposed to play fair and when somebody crosses the line and does something unfair to you, you have to stand up for yourself because otherwise people will keep on taking advantage of you and step all over you, like people used to do to her when she was young and before she learned to stand up for herself, which believe me, is completely impossible to imagine now. My mom is a social worker at the domestic crisis center and she deals with really messed up kids every day. She is right down on the dirty floor, Journal. She's a fighter. That is my mom.

That is one way that she is different from Renata's mom, whose name is Magdalena Le Cortez, who is a famous artist and whose number one rule in life is: *ignore all the ordinary people*. Renata said that her mother is a successful artist because she has mastered this rule.

It is not a terribly helpful rule for a girl in junior high who is being slowly driven insane by evil boys, but I guess it worked really well for Magdalena, until she was in a terrible car accident in Charlotte, West Virginia, three years ago. She almost died. Now she walks with a cane and can't go up or down stairs. She has beautiful black hair and she always wears amazing clothes and silver jewelry from Mexico, but when she walks across the room, it's like suddenly she's eighty years old. Her whole body shakes with each step. And Renata says she's very self-conscious about her limp, so she hardly ever goes anywhere but instead stays in her mansion on top of Dewey Hill and paints and paints and paints. It is so high up in the dunes that nobody even knows there's a house up there. She paints in a huge all-glass studio. Did I mention that she is a Surrealist? I didn't even know what a Surrealist was until I met Renata. Can you even imagine what it would be like to tell people that your mom is a Surrealist?

When Renata first took us home with her after school in December, we were out-of-our-minds impressed. I was trying to act normal, but Nate was having fits behind Renata's back, rolling his eyes, dropping his jaw, smacking his forehead. The house is around seventy years old, designed by this famous Chicago architect and HUGE, HUGE, HUGE! Did I mention huge? There are three levels, each one big enough to be a normal-sized house. Mr. Le Cortez lives on the top level; Magdalena has the ground-level (no stairs); and Renata has basically the entire finished basement. She doesn't have her own room, Journal, she has her own level. She has modern furniture that she picked out from a CATALOG and it was DELIVERED to her PRIVATE ENTRANCE. I am not even exaggerating.

Does it sound like I'm really materialistic? I'm not. And Nate is the most non-materialistic person I know—all he cares about is writing and books and watching anime cartoons. He doesn't even own a cell phone. He doesn't even have a laptop. He likes writing things out longhand. He says it's more pure.

You have to remember that when Renata took us to her house, we had recently been stung at our school and were invisible. So a beautiful mansion on a hidden road in the dunes was a miracle, something out of a fairy tale, something that gave us hope. After we met Renata, and started spending time at her mansion, we began to feel lucky again. We grew stronger from her pure energy and her talent. And braver, too, much braver. Brave enough to believe we could stop Chase Dobson.

Nate calls his mother Sylvia, Journal. He won't call her Mom. She is a religious fanatic. Nate says that sometimes he hears her praying for him in her bedroom. When she prays, she doesn't call him Nate, she calls him "my first-born." *Please help my firstborn find his way back to your light.* Nate has a sister who is a year younger than him and his mom had twins five years later—two hyper boys—and a few years after that her husband moved to Ohio, where he is supposedly some top executive for a company and someday soon he will move his family to Cleveland, but Nate promised me he won't go. His dad sends money every month and Sylvia is constantly packing for the big move. That, and doing laundry. And prayers. And naps, lots of naps. She sleeps all the time and Nate's sister basically takes care of the twins. So Nate is completely on his own. He is free, Journal. Freer than I will ever be.

Whenever I go over there—which isn't very often because Nate never wants to be home—his mom is in her bedroom, either sleeping or praying. She takes Xanax and Ambien every single day. Nate showed me the prescriptions. He said that they were basically to help her cope with having a non-believer for a son. After he said this, he lifted one eyebrow high, clear up halfway into his forehead. I love it when he does that; it's brilliant.

One time my mom told me never to trust a man who does not respect his mother. Mom says things like this sometimes, like she has all this inner wisdom about men, even though I have never known her to even go out on a date. So I am skeptical. I reminded her that my best friend in the world does not respect his mother very much.

Mom: For Nate I will make an exception.

Me: Why? Have you met his mother? (She does hear lots of inside gossip about our town from her job at the Domestic Crisis Center.)

11

Mom: Never met her.

Me: Then why did you say that?

Mom: (No answer.)

*Me: So does that rule about respecting your mom apply
    to girls too?*

Mom: Oh Sweetie, girls are different.

I should mention here that my mom thinks she knows everything there is to know about girls. From her job. She's like a guru of screwed-up girls.

*Mom: Respect comes and goes, in and out the window
    like air, ever-changing, shades of gray, dust in the
    wind. And I think you know exactly what I mean,
    big girl.*

She has called me her big girl ever since I was seven. And she was right, Journal; I did know what she meant. Nate loves my mom and wishes he had a mom like her, but he doesn't know how hard it is to have your entire family be just your mom. A mom who is obsessed with you. I need my space, Journal, and she is always in my space. Plus Nate has never seen her explode at me like she did that one time about the Lucky Charms on the floor. Like an insane woman, seriously. Or last night when she visited me in juvie and completely lost it in the visiting room in front of all the other visitors and sobbed really REALLY loud for a whole hour.

It was hard to get positive after she left and it is so important to stay positive in here.

I don't blame her for being mad at me, but you should know, Journal, that I was partly protecting her. I don't want anything else bad to happen to her. She always said, Katie, hold your head up and don't be a victim and never be sorry for who you are. Hear me now, Journal, just hear me now! No matter how long I have to be a prisoner in here, away from my mom and my friends, I will never be sorry for who I am! Never, never, never. I did what I had to do for Renata and Nate!

I got through all of it—that awful thing they called arraignment and that even worse thing they called intake and then my first night in the slammer with that scary loud CLANG and then that really loud BUZZ that the doors make once you are locked in—it makes you feel like you'll never get out alive!

And then that horrible first night on that horrible bed in that horrible room with a toilet right out in the open and a window so high up on the wall you can only see the sky and nothing else, and then they lock you in for the night and some total stranger can check on you through a little window in the door. They check on you every fifteen minutes, Journal! They watch you all the time. I'm in Pod A with seven other girls and only one of them is being friendly to me. Her name is Rosie. Maybe they're a little afraid of me because I'm tall, I don't know. Renata was never afraid of me, even though I towered over her. She is so small. I miss her so much.

I don't see how she can survive in here, sleeping in a room that is about as big as one of her closets, wearing ugly old sweats and eating terrible food. She feels things more deeply than most people. She is special that way. I have to be strong for her. I have to be strong for Nate too, because I promised him I would be strong. And I can do it, Journal. I am not who I was before all this happened, before I did what I did to protect my friends. I am in juvie! I'm really here! I am locked up for real in Ferndale Juvie and nobody can get me out!

It's getting dark outside. There is a little window over my bed that shows the sky. They will take my pen and lock me in my room soon, but I can take it. I can do it. I am First GreyMount Katie!

Nathaniel, Son of James

June 8
Day Two of Captivity

Evening: When I arrived in the Hall of Lost Souls, I bravely stood with my GreyMounts, one on either side of me, and as three, we faced our accusers. Bravely, impassively, we heard the words that foretold our imprisonment. We stood united, and we did not falter, and we shed not one tear among us. Then we were led away in silence, a dark, unbroken silence. We walked down a Corridor of Doom into a small and terrible room, and in this room we were put into cages, interrogated, and examined. In this room, we came to know what would happen to us—our separation. Before I entered the terrible room, wherein I was torn from my true sisters, I saw them for the last time, my brave GreyMounts. We fell upon one another and without words renewed our vows with our eyes. We sent rays of strength into each other's hearts, and we remained as one, though it was clear that we would not be together, as we had hoped. We would henceforth be kept far apart, farther than we had ever thought possible in the days before our imprisonment.

Now I am alone and unarmed, Great She, stripped of my ancestry and banished from my village. I am a prisoner, yet I am not bowed, and I am not tamed, and I fear not further punishment, nor isolation, nor banishment, for I am Nathaniel, Chief GreyMount, firstborn, swordsman of the Clan of the Danes, cage-dweller, scribe and messenger, eldest son of James of Cleves, who guides my hand from afar.

As you have requested, I shall speak of the events which ended the cruel attacks on my second GreyMount, events which required all of my wits and my strength and courage, and in the end, led me to this place of mortification. To this end, I shall tell what I am able of my earliest memories of our enemy, the Master of Contortions. My ordeal began during my Year of Watchfulness, during which I spoke to almost no one, and during which my solitary path intersected only with the path of my first GreyMount, a warrior of great height and silent strength. This was before the arrival of my second GreyMount, who came from Southern regions, where she learned sorcery from her mother, whose paintings are filled with strange magic.

I am tall, Great She, taller than the Master of Contortions, yet my strength is not readily apparent to most eyes. Only my GreyMounts saw me clearly for who I was. Their faith in my powers gave me the courage I needed to face my enemy and secure the Master's capture.

United, we waited for the exact moment of our ascendancy, which required stealth and silence and extreme loyalty. And we succeeded! We acted as one and brought about the deliverance of the Master, even as it also led me and my comrades to this fortress of isolation and sleeplessness, far from everything that is familiar.

In the Place of Contrition, I am allowed to read or to write only until the hour of absolute confinement, when all doors are locked and all hope is gone. There is nothing to do but close my eyes and disappear into the night in my cell.

June 9
Day Three of Captivity

Morning: You asked me about the beginnings of my ordeal and so I will start with the first memories of my enemy, The Master of Contortions, he who today weighs heavily on my thoughts. He is a great warrior in his own right, raised for glory and fame by his parents, who were among the nobility of our region. His father, an overseer of the Great Hall of North Holmes, christened the boy in his own name and the name of his father before him and guided him throughout childhood in the art of warfare.

His mother, although bitterly disappointed in her own ambitions, also aspired to greatness and made certain that her only son wore the mantle of ascendancy. His prowess in games and competitions grew and his feats were known far and wide. Fierce and long-limbed, the master could run for hours without the slightest sign of weariness. On fields and in arenas, his rivals and enemies of all ages already feared his name, though he had lived but thirteen summers.

The Great Hall was filled with legions of his admirers. Beautiful maidens awaited his attention. But alas, in his heart was a great and spreading doubt that caused him to abuse himself, and it reduced his power to shallow acts of cruelty. He began to find pleasure in various persecutions. He relished all opportunities to bring humiliation and fear to those who were not among his admirers. His soul darkened.

All of this I learned in the Year of My Watchfulness, my apprenticeship, before my first GreyMount joined me.

You asked me to write about my home life, but there is little to say about my blood family, Great She. My quest is unrelated to the accident of my birth. I would rather that you see me as I am in my present circumstance— exiled, without family, without homeland, without armor. I am Nathaniel, prince of dangerous journeys. My father, once king, has wandered far from me. Long ago, before my time, my mother bewitched him. Now she is a fading shadow, a wraith whose life is becoming more and more of a waking dream. Soon only my shadow-sister will be able to see her. To my smaller brothers, she will become completely invisible. My shadow-sister shares a likeness with me, but she does not have my courage nor my thirst for justice. She is ignorant of my quest. In the Great Halls, she turned from me, averted her eyes and pretended not to know me when our paths crossed. This caused me pain until I found my true sisters.

They are my only family now, Great She, and I will not betray them, no matter what further tribulations await me in my vigil in Pod B, with seven other male prisoners and Carl, the Prison Steward, none of whom can help me. They don't know me, and I don't know them. They don't understand what I have done, nor why, nor how. No one here can understand the torments of my secret heart.

Social Worker

Thursday, June 10

On the social worker's desk was a stack of folders, an open laptop, a cup of herbal tea with vitamin C, and a new box of aloe-infused Kleenex. Greta Shield sipped her bitter tea and coughed, softly but miserably, into a Kleenex held to her mouth. In the stuffed chair beside her desk sat one of the three new residents—Renata Le Cortez, her forehead resting on her knees. Her short hair was matted at the back of her head, awry on the top with two thin strands on either side of her head to her shoulders. Her small shoulders were shaking. She was soundlessly weeping.

They were halfway through a particularly difficult preliminary interview—difficult in part because it was three days overdue. The social worker had seen the two other residents first and then become sick enough to miss two days of work and necessarily postpone her first meeting with Renata until that morning. As luck would have it, this girl, the youngest and smallest of the three new residents, was much more traumatized to be in juvenile detention than either of her friends. She looked more like a distraught fifth-grade boy than a girl in junior high, especially because the red sweats she was wearing were far too big and baggy for her tiny frame. She had already used and discarded several dozen Kleenexes.

Greta felt guilty. It was not unusual for a female offender to cry during the first meeting, but Renata's distress was disconcerting because of her size. She spoke through her tears with unusual formality and a slight, uncategorizable accent. This, and her messy hair, made her seem particularly fragile and slightly exotic, like a sick tropical bird. On her laptop the social worker typed in caps: *MAKE APPT. W/ PSYCH. ASAP.*

The folders on her desk contained the police reports. These included an overview of the kidnapping charges and the subsequent arrests. Greta opened the first folder with one hand, pressing a Kleenex to her nose. The report stated that on Friday, May 28, Chase Dobson had been taken from a party by the three accused, in a severely compromised, drug- and alcohol-induced state, driven to the home of Renata Le Cortez on Prospect Street in North Holmes, and imprisoned there for one week. The house's owners, Magdalena and Stefano Le Cortez, had moved to North Holmes less than a year before and claimed total ignorance of the fact that a well-known boy had been held against his will in the lower level of their home. The police report stated that Xanax, Adderall, and Oxycontin had been routinely administered by Dobson's captors, and that as a result the victim had been unable to attempt escape for the duration of his captivity.

According to the same report:

> *Minors taken into custody on June 7. None responded to charges at their Prelim Hearing; Juvenile Court Referee found probable cause for detention based on the accusations of the victim and the police statement. Minors were then admitted to the JDC, where they will be held for assessment after an inconclusive adjudication hearing.*

The social worker closed the police report folder and opened the folder underneath, the intake results for the three residents. These reported no health issues, no substance abuse issues, no suicide ideation, and no known recent trauma for any of the three. But Renata was clearly miserable, and the social worker was sorry that she had not been able to see this obviously more needy girl until several days into her incarceration. According to Dan, the shift supervisor, she was barely eating, not speaking, not sleeping well, and not functioning academically, despite a 4.0 GPA in the eighth grade. Worst of all, the need to separate her from her two friends had necessitated placing her into Pod C, the younger boys' pod, where three upper-elementary boys were currently residing. Apparently, according to Dan, Renata was generally refusing to communicate with anyone in the pod and was spending all of her personal time in her room with the door closed. Dan had also requested that she see the staff psychologist. No family members had yet visited.

The social worker coughed into her hand a few times and then cleared her throat. "Is there anything else you want to talk to me about today?" she asked Renata. "We still have a little time before you have to go back to your classroom."

Renata took a new Kleenex, wiped her tears, and blew her nose. "I need my own things around me," she said. "Please. I need my bathrobe. I need my clothes."

"I understand how you feel about the regulation clothes. I wish it wasn't a requirement. But I'm afraid I can't change this for you."

"When can I see my friends, Mrs. Shield?"

"You know that isn't possible either, Renata."

"Why can't I just talk to them for a few minutes? Or at least see them. I need to see Katie."

"If you're worried about her, I can tell you that she's doing fine. Both your friends are fine. I plan to meet with them later today."

"We didn't know it was going to be like this. We thought we'd be in here together. We thought we'd be able to . . . take care of each other. Like at school."

"You can take care of each other. You can tell me exactly how all of this happened. How it started and all of the events leading up to your arrest."

Renata lowered her head back onto the top of her knees, refusing to speak.

"Listen to me now. I'm really sorry that I wasn't able to be here for you when you first arrived. I know you've had a tough couple of days, and I promise I'll make it up to you. But there is something I need you to do for me. I need you to keep a journal, starting today."

Renata's demeanor changed. She sat up straight. She lowered her bare feet to the floor and slipped them back into her scuffs. "I like that idea very much," she said. "Very much. Would the paper in my journal need to be lined paper?"

"That is entirely up to you. I just need you to tell me in your own words how all of this started."

"I prefer no lines. Or holes in the paper. Or spiral binders. Would you be the one picking out the journals, Mrs. Shield? Like at an office supply store? Because I would really and truly prefer one with a hard cover and heavy white paper."

"Do you mean more like a sketchbook?"

The girl nodded hopefully.

"Well . . . I can probably find something like that for you, if you promise to use it every day."

"Oh, I'll use it, Mrs. Shield."

"I want you to explain how this started, Renata. I want to hear about the events leading up to the night you and your friends took Chase to your house. Eventually you will need to make a statement based on your recollections— something official for your court date later this month."

"Will anyone besides you see my journal?"

"Only me."

"You won't show the journal to my mother?"

"Absolutely not."

Renata sat back in the chair again and sighed. "Have you met my mother?"

"Not yet. I've been too sick. But I will be doing that today." She glanced at the clock. "We have ten minutes, Renata. Is there anything else you want to tell me?"

"I don't belong in a pod with boys, Mrs. Shield."

"I'm very sorry that you were put in Pod C. Dan and I will do whatever we can to correct the situation. And I will arrange to meet your parents as soon as possible."

"My mother is an artist," Renata reported sadly. "She was rather well known back in Charlotte. She owned her own gallery there. It was called Animal Dreams."

"I see. And was it difficult for you, Renata, leaving Charlotte, coming to a strange school where you didn't know a single soul?"

"It was until I found my friends. Katie and Nate—they accepted me. They are beyond friends. They wouldn't let those boys continue hurting me."

"I know that boys can be very cruel in junior high. But can you tell me whose idea it was to retaliate by keeping Chase a prisoner at your house?"

Renata withdrew, drawing her spine back into the chair. She closed her eyes. "Have you also asked my friends to keep journals?" she asked softly.

"Yes, I have."

"And they said they would do it?"

The social worker leaned forward in her chair, moving her body closer to Renata's, extending her arm closer to Renata's leg, but being careful not to touch her. "Let me explain something important to you. I am not asking you or your friends to keep journals in a way where you would be free to say no. You are all in a great deal of trouble. The charges against you are serious. It is very important that you cooperate with me. This journal is something I am requiring. And in doing so, I am also presenting you with a way to both prepare for your day in court and to begin your rehabilitation."

As she spoke, Renata began visibly crumbling again, her mouth trembling, her feet coming back up from the floor. She clutched her knees and tightened her arms around them and began rocking slightly. "I need my friends," she said. "I need my own things. My mind is all jumbled in here."

She dropped her head and began to weep again, a faint, childlike sound that made the social worker feel again as if she was dealing with someone too young to be in juvenile detention. She glanced at the clock on her desk—their time was up. "I know how much you miss your friends," she said quietly. "I'm going to help you. I promise."

She began stacking the folders on her desk, signaling to Renata that their session was ending. The social worker told the girl that sometime later in the day, a staff member would deliver a sketchbook—hard black cover, no holes, no lines, no spiral—and that she should ask Dan for a pen or pencil, whenever she was free to write. She was to write only during personal time and only when her homework was finished.

"I do thank you so very much, Mrs. Shield," Renata said, holding a fresh Kleenex against the side of her mottled face.

The social worker hid her surprise. It was unusual for a resident to thank her, much less at a first meeting.

Alone, she turned to her laptop. "Atypical detainee," she typed. "Really struggling. Needs to be relocated ASAP. Additional therapy recommended. Probably sleep deprived. Why no visitors?"

She added a smattering of notes:

Renata Le Cortez: First Meeting: Small for her age, unusually formal, extremely emotional. Tendency to speak with polite affectation, which may be a mask. Check with staff, teachers, med personnel. How to help this girl?

Subsequently she read over the notes she had scribbled three days earlier, the day she'd left her office early, already under the influence of a powerful strain of summer flu.

> Katie Havenga: <u>First Meeting</u>: Calm, not hostile, good eye contact, no tears. Single parent family. Says her mother is a social worker too—check on this. Seems intelligent, probably a good student. Accepting of incarceration. Aware of the seriousness of the situation. Expressed no regret, except for being worried about the other female resident.
>
> Nate Wilson: <u>First Meeting</u>: Eldest child, one sister, twin brothers, father relocated to Cleveland for economic reasons. Could explain air of melancholy. No history of violence or substance abuse. Cooperative yet reserved. Poor eye contact. Unusually polite. Depressed?

The social worker opened a new file and titled it <u>Post First Meeting Goals</u>:

> Establish the sequence of events leading up to the kidnapping. No contact allowed among the three residents. Each will keep a daily journal to both reflect on his/her situation and to record, in his/her own words, the events leading up to the crime. Hopefully the residents will feel more free to confide in writing

about motivation and intent. Many questions about the guilt/ innocence of these teenagers. Undeniable withholding of information. Absence of guilt or regret seems out of kilter with the fact that not one of them has ever been in trouble before. Yet all three acting somewhat hardened in their unwillingness to talk to me.

Wilson and Havenga seem aware that a serious line was crossed; in particular the boy used language indicating that he understood that his behavior had been criminal. Havenga seems too smart not to understand what it means to be in juvenile detention. She admitted during our second interview that she and her friends had made a "mistake."

Here the social worker stopped, blew her nose a few times to clear her head, and played back a portion of the video she had made of her first session with Katie Havenga. Unlike Renata, Katie sat tall and straight-backed in the meeting room chair, hands settled in her lap, sweating profusely, but appearing calm.

Date: Tuesday, June 7

First Interview with Katie Havenga

From the videotape:

GS: So you admit you and your friends made a mistake?

KH: [Tugging nervously on her lower lip] Okay, wait. The idea itself wasn't a mistake. Just . . . like the way it happened turned it into a mistake.

GS: I'm not sure what you mean, Katie. The idea to kidnap Chase Dobson wasn't a mistake?

KH: To you it might seem like one. But to us . . . we were just trying to stop him from being so . . . evil. We just . . . we had to stop him.

GS: If you had to stop him, then what part of what you did seems like a mistake?

KH: [Uncomfortable] That it went on so long.

GS: Katie, Chase's statement alleges that you and your friends made him take prescription tranquilizers while he was locked in the laundry room at Renata's house.

KH: I don't want to talk about that.

GS: Katie . . .

KH: No, I don't want to. Maybe next time.

GS: Can I at least assume that you are experiencing some regret about how you and your friends chose to deal with Chase Dobson?

KH: I wouldn't exactly call it regret. I don't like it here, and I'm really worried about Renata, and I want to go home, but I don't regret what we did. It was for Renata. How can I regret doing something for my best friend when she needed me to do it?

GS: Hmmm. Okay. So you mentioned . . . you said . . . you consider Chase Dobson to be an evil person?

KH: Everybody knows he's evil, Mrs. Shield. Lots of kids are afraid of him. Even some teachers are afraid of him.

GS: But had you at any time considered another way of dealing with his bullying?

[Silence]

GS: Surely you don't need me to list for you all of the things you and your friends could have done instead of what you actually did. Surely you are aware of all of the people you could have turned to for help—teachers, aides, school counselors, the assistant principal . . .

KH: No one helps kids like us, Mrs. Shield. Not at my school. We aren't the important kids. Not even Nate and he's like a genius. We knew it wouldn't stop unless we stopped it ourselves.

[End of videotape]

No one helps kids like us. Katie had said this thoughtfully, without bitterness. The social worker was also struck by how carefully the girl had chosen her words, weighing them before each statement. When their hour was up, she'd exhaled noisily and left the room almost at a run, obviously relieved to be finished, as though she had passed some sort of crucial test.

The social worker clicked open her file on Nate Wilson. She felt that there was no point in examining the video of his first meeting, since he had said so little. She hoped that he would make a real effort in his journal. He seemed capable of it, almost eager to begin. He had also left her office in a relieved rush. But then he'd stopped at the door, leaned back into the room in his faded green sweats and his shapeless scuffs, one long arm stretching up, touching the top of the doorframe, and he asked her if she would please, from now on, call him *Nathaniel*.

Remembering this, the social worker deleted *Nate* as the title on the file and renamed his file *Nathaniel*.

First GreyMount Katie

If only Chase had left her alone, Journal. If only he had picked on some other girl—me, for instance, me who had already been stung, who had nowhere further down to go. I'm not afraid of boys. I would have walked up to those creeps. I would have walked up to Chase himself. I would have looked him in the eye and stood like a statue, like steel, and he is the one who would have backed down, Journal, I'm sure of it. I know his kind—he's a coward inside. He would have seen that I was not a girl he could bully. I am a GreyMount. Chase and his friends would have backed away from me, although it wouldn't have stopped them, not really. They would've just found some other girl in some other school hallway, made her life hell for the fun of it. God, I hate boys like that, Journal, they are so awful and so stupid, bloodsucking jerks with their ugly, dead hearts and their tiny dinosaur brains.

But he didn't go after another girl, Journal. He went after my friend. And his goons followed along with it because he is their leader. And it hurt her so much. It changed her. She is sensitive, Journal. She is kind. She's an artist like her mother and she went to a private school in Charlotte where stuff like this doesn't happen. She is not used to a place like North Holmes. She did not know about the meanness of boys who think they are already so important just because they are jocks, boys who think they can do anything and no one will stop them, and no one does stop them, not even the teachers who see what they do every day.

Chase is important at my school, Journal—he plays soccer, basketball, and tennis—and he is the best player on every team he is on. He probably already has college sports scholarships and he's not even in high school yet. Plus his father is on the school board, which I know only because my mom complains about it all the time; she says the Dobsons think they own the public schools in North Holmes. And Chase's mother once ran for mayor of North Holmes, like two years ago, but she didn't win. My mom didn't vote for her even though she was a woman and she usually votes for the women. This was because Mom worked with her once on a committee to help pregnant girls finish high school and Mom said Lenora Dobson was a snob AND a bore and those are her two biggest put-downs in the world.

Nate was over to my house, having lunch with me when she said this about Chase's mom. He gave me one of his *I love your mom* looks, but now as I'm writing this, Journal, I am realizing—we were talking about Lenora Dobson way back before Chase even started hurting Renata. I think this might have even been before either one of us even met Renata. Why were we talking about Chase's mother back then? I am wracking my brain to remember. I think Nate might have asked me a question about Chase, like I would know who he was, but now I can't remember what the question was. The only thing I knew about Chase Dobson back then was that he was king of our school. I didn't even know he HAD a mother.

My mom was eavesdropping, like she always did whenever Nate was over, butting in with some comment or other, trying to sound like she is so cool. That day she asked us if we were talking about Lenora Dobson's kid.

Nate said yes, like it was something he totally already knew—that Chase Dobson was Lenora Dobson's kid. And then Mom butted even more into our conversation and told us the part about being on a committee with Lenora Dobson and how she was a snob and a bore and didn't understand teenagers at all and thought she was the mayor of North Holmes, even though she didn't win the election.

Here's something I don't know, Journal—why was Nate thinking about Chase, asking about him, way back then, *months* before we got stung, *months* before Chase went after Renata? I need to ask him! Nate—can you hear me? Nate—my first best friend, Nate! Where are you right now? Are you okay? Are they letting you write your stories? I know it would be so awful for you if they don't let you write.

BUT WHY WERE YOU ASKING QUESTIONS ABOUT CHASE BACK THEN BACK BEFORE ANY OF THIS STARTED?

I don't get it. I don't get it. But I have to stop writing. I have to go to class.

Journal Entry June 9—After Gym

All my classes are finished. They give us homework and writing assignments in here, Journal, but the homework is easy, easier than regular school—I can do my homework assignments in like twenty minutes, and then I'm free to read and write in my journal until dinner.

I have now been here for four days, four days without being able to see or talk to my friends. That is definitely the worst part of being in here, Journal. One time we passed Nate's pod in the hall on the way to the gym. That isn't supposed to happen, so the boy's pod had to face the wall because we are not supposed to make eye contact with the other pods in the hall. So when I passed Nate, he was facing the wall and all I could see was his back. The back of his head was all snarly and flat and usually it isn't like that—he has beautiful hair. I don't even know if he saw me before he turned to the wall. I don't know what he was thinking. I felt ashamed, but I don't know why. That was my worst moment so far, Journal. Worse than when I first went through intake and Lee Ann checked my head for lice. She shined a light on my head, looking for lice, I swear to God. And then I had to take off all my clothes and take a shower and Lee Ann was right there and it wasn't private and I knew that Nate and Renata were locked in these little rooms nearby and they were going to have to do the exact same thing after me, but we couldn't see each other to let each other know that we survived it.

And while I was in the shower I thought about Renata getting her head checked for lice, and I started to cry with my head turned to the tiles so that Lee Ann couldn't see my face and for a few minutes I wasn't First GreyMount Katie. I was just Katie and I was for real in juvie and I wasn't sure I was going to be able to stand it. And that was even before I knew that I wasn't going to see my friends at all, ever. Not even for five minutes a day. But then I turned to steel again, and nobody in here has ever seen me cry, and nobody ever will.

I don't think Renata can do it! I don't think she will last. She isn't strong like me! I can't even picture her on the bed that is really just a cement cot that comes out of the wall with the world's thinnest mattress and the world's scratchiest blanket, and I can't picture her in her pod and getting locked into her room at night, and I can't picture her being forced to go to gym class twice a day (she hates all sports!) and I can't picture her taking a shower with no good hair products, and I can't picture her wearing horrible sweats and the old worn out, stretched out, stained underwear that they give you in here. I know Nate can do it, because he is Nate, but I don't see how Renata is going to be able to stand it, and I don't know what that means for the pact! I can't think of one single way to help her.

I miss them so much, Journal. I miss them so much that I have to stop writing. I have to close my notebook. I have to get calm again, breathing deep like my mom does when she has to get calm after a bad day at work. I have to get calm and not cry. Get calm and not cry. I am First GreyMount. I am First GreyMount. I am First GreyMount.

Journal Entry Friday, June 10—Personal Time

Today I realized something. Something really big. I realized that there is no way I am going to be able to show Mrs. Shield my journal! I can't! It's too late! I've already put way too much private stuff, even though I haven't actually written down what really happened.

The thing is I NEED to write in a journal. I need to write. I guess I better get another journal, so I have two, one for Mrs. Shield and one just for me. I have to somehow get another one.

Because I really do need to keep writing about all the things I can't ever tell Mrs. Shield. I really do need to remember. I need to get all the facts clear in my head. I need truth, Journal, I need to surround myself with truth. I need to write down all my questions and my piled up secrets and my worrying about Renata or I will never be able to last in here and keep the pact.

It is after lunchtime now, and I am in the day room, and I feel stronger today. I feel like I can do this. And I know that Nate can do it too. He is so amazing and wise. But, oh, Renata, my perfect and beautiful friend, please stay strong and don't crack and don't betray the pact and don't tell!

 # nathaniel, Son of James

Journal

Day Four of Captivity

Evening: In the winter of my Watchfulness, I saw that the Master carried with him a silver flask. He poured from the flask often, into a bottle of strengthening beverage. The flask was an heirloom handed down from his grandfather, whose death at sea was a bitter loss. The Master readily combined the contents of this silver heirloom with his athletic drink in the Great Halls and the open fields and the midnight gatherings of his warriors. His partaking of the special potion grew more and more frequent; the flask moved more carelessly from hip to hand to bottle to lips and was easily observed by me in my Year of Watchfulness. But it also came to my attention that the potion did not calm the Master, nor bring warmth to his voice, nor gentleness to his manner, but rather increased his need to spread fear.

This perplexed me mightily, Great She. Why was the Master so cruel? I saw that he took special pleasure in these attacks, far out of proportion to their rewards. The incidents often occurred after a day where the flashing of his grandfather's flask was most noticeable and where several of his consorts were invited to also partake of the potion, firing their blood. Together they formed a wall and attacked with much mirth and pageantry. Among the unfortunates afflicted with these cruel attentions were Andrea Froelich, Jane Messinger, and Della Ruspino—she in particular who might also have become one of my sisters had she not despaired and nearly extinguished herself and then transferred to a Great Hall in a neighboring village. The other victims remained, ghostlike, never to fully recover from their time of torment.

All of this I watched from afar, helpless to stem the tide of malice from the Master. That was my stance, an invisible stance, until one of my own sisters came under attack.

There are other things I must reveal. And I will speak of them upon the morrow. The Prison Steward has announced that my time of writing is over. I must return my pen and keep my silence. Soon I will be locked into the chamber and made to sleep under the watching eyes of strangers.

Journal
Day Five of Captivity

Morning: I have been a prisoner in the Place of Contrition for five days, and I have tried to write for you as diligently as time permits, for the days are filled with scheduled challenges and forced confinements and restrictions. The times when I can write most freely are the evenings. I have asked the prison steward if I might be allowed to write late into the night, in my solitary cave. He says not without special permission and that he would put in a request for it to my shift supervisor, but that he would probably say no. So I am today mentally preparing to convince him—to entreat him for special permission to do what I was born to do—write. Perhaps you could convince the shift supervisor—his name is Chad, Great She, and I believe that you have great powers of influence in the Place of Contrition. Perhaps from reading my journal, you will see that describing the great and tragic defeats, as well as the most thrilling victories of my GreyMounts, is both my calling and the wellspring of my sanity.

I have sensed curiosity from my brethren in captivity about the reasons for my imprisonment, and yet I am unable to reveal the details of my crime, both because of the oath I took with my GreyMounts and because of my suspicion that my fellow prisoners would not understand the powerful under forces that have led me from the battlefield to this place, where no one knows me and where no one can help me. In fact, there are many things about me that the seven other prisoners would not comprehend—my loyalties, my refusal to reveal myself during the Time of Forced Revelations, my lack of contrition for my crime, my longing for books and paper and a proper pen to relieve my suffering, my estrangement from the family of my birth—excluding my devotion to my father, the exiled James of Cleves of the Clan of the Danes, whose spirit lives in me.

I have this morning a great longing to see my first GreyMount, she who has known me the longest, she who is stout of heart, long of limb, and loyal beyond words. When I first was drawn to her in the Great Hall, one year ago, I saw how bravely she walked through the same place that had become a place of fear for me, and so I chose her, Great She. I saw in her great nobility, both in her carriage and her gaze. Sometimes I would watch her coming toward me in the Hall, and I would admire how she moved as though no one could distract or divert her. She is fine, Great She. She is fortunate. She has a mother who raised her to be a secret warrior.

Sometimes in times of duress, my first GreyMount would lament about her mother, the one who bore her and raised her alone, imparting great wisdom in a world filled with falsity and deception and cruelty. My Grey-Mount's mother is a champion of female changelings. She rescues the ghosts who wander the Great Hall and the streets of my village without protection. She is the Lady of Forgotten Girls and in this, she is as noble as the noblest leaders of North Holmes. More noble, in fact, because she works in the hidden rooms and neighborhoods of our village. And she sees me and accepts me as I am. She always has a smile and a word of kindness for me, the Forgotten Boy, and she is among the few who know the side of me that is Nathaniel.

If only my own mother had some of this lady's courage and wisdom, Great She! Would I still have ended up here, in this place? If only the one who bore me had one-tenth of the wisdom of the Lady of Forgotten Girls! If only she was not paralyzed in the darkness of her bedroom, a prisoner in the cage of her own making! If only James of Cleves had not left me behind with her. If he had taken me with him, I would have guided his hand as he has guided mine. We could have escaped together.

My time for writing is up, Great She. The next test of my endurance awaits me.

Social Worker

Friday, June 11

Katie's mother was waiting in the reception area, wearing black jeans and a white peasant tunic, looking far too young to be a social worker or to have a daughter Katie's age. Greta shook Claire Havenga's hand. "Mrs. Havenga, I was just about to call you."

She escorted her guest through steel security doors, back to her office. As they walked, the social worker realized something else about the woman—she had seen her before. She searched her mind as she walked and it came to her—Claire Havenga—of course! A social worker who, like herself, specialized in working with female juveniles! The social worker flashed back to a conference in Lansing a couple of years before—a special weekend for professionals, the third annual Reclaiming Girls Conference. Claire Havenga of the Odetta County Domestic Crisis Center was keynote speaker.

Unlike the other parents involved, Claire Havenga had visited her daughter every evening since Katie had become a resident. The word from staff was that Katie endured these visits from her mother, but clearly would have preferred to see her less often. Each morning since the social worker's illness, she'd found messages and memos from the day and night staff *Mrs. Havenga requests a meeting ASAP about Katie.*

"Mrs. Havenga, I'm so sorry that it has taken me this long to meet with you. You probably heard that I was gone because I've been very . . . "

"Sick—I know. The staff told me." She set a tote bag on the floor and closed her eyes tightly. "I stopped every morning on my way to work. But now that I'm here, finally talking to you, I don't know where to begin. I'm so upset. I'm just so upset. I've been here four days in a row and I still can't believe this is happening! Every time I walk through the doors, every time I get ID'd and wanded, I feel like I must be dreaming."

"I can request that you not be wanded, Mrs. Havenga, if that would help you."

In reply, Claire picked up her bag from the floor and began rummaging through it, finding a business card and setting it on the desk between them. The social worker studied the card politely, although she had already known what it would say:

Claire R. Havenga
Teen Advocate
Domestic Crisis Center of North Holmes

"I work with girls," Claire said. Then, as though this information implied a deep personal failure, her composure completely crumbled. "I'm sorry. I'm sorry. I'm having a really hard time with this."

"I understand, Mrs. Havenga. It must be very difficult, given your profession, to have your own daughter..."

"I just can't get *through* to her! She won't *talk* to me! And she's always been able to tell me *anything*! What changed? What happened to her? How could she have done something so...something so..." She covered her mouth with one hand in horror and finished, "*prolonged!*"

"I'm working very hard to earn Katie's trust so that she will tell me exactly what happened. I lost a little time, getting sick when I did, but right now, working with these kids is my absolute number one priority."

Claire responded by breaking down, much the way Renata Le Cortez had broken down in the same chair, the day before. The social worker glanced at the clock and pushed the Kleenex box closer to the edge of her desk.

"Mrs. Havenga," she said. "I want you to feel free to come and talk to me again, but I'm afraid I have a staff meeting very shortly and . . . "

Claire lifted a streaked face. "Can you imagine how humiliating this is for me?" After a pause, she asked plaintively, "Is that a really selfish thing to say?"

"No, but . . . "

"There are people right now who are saying this happened because I give so much attention to my clients that I couldn't see what was happening in my own home. People wait for this sort of thing, Greta. May I call you Greta?"

The social worker nodded and chose her words carefully. "I don't necessarily think this happened because you weren't paying attention to your daughter. But I must confess that I don't yet understand why it did happen. And I urgently need to understand why. It's my number one priority today to . . . "

"She's a *good girl*!" Claire cried. "A beautiful person. And so is Nate. I love that boy so much! He's not a criminal! None of them belong here. But least of all Katie."

After she pronounced her daughter's name, she clamped one hand over her mouth, holding back the next wave of sobs. The social worker took this opportunity to stand up and come out from behind her desk. She put a hand on Claire's shoulder and leaned in, promising to meet with her again, first thing Monday morning. Claire stood up and gathered her things. She let herself be led back to the security entrance, one hand still covering her mouth.

. . .

None of the other parents had responded to the social worker's meeting requests. This happened occasionally with repeat offenders, the sort of residents whose parents or guardians had given up on them, but it was unusual for first-timers, especially first-timers who had never been in any sort of trouble before. The social worker made a note to call both Magdalena Le Cortez and Sylvia Wilson again before the end of the day. She also canceled a meeting later in the day with the court-appointed lawyer for Katie and Nathaniel. She needed more face-time with each resident.

She glanced at the clock. Nearly time for the Friday staff meeting, but she had an impulse to quickly make one more call—to the parents of Chase Dobson. She left a voice mail at their home, explaining who she was and urging one or both of them to meet with her. "I hope to learn more about Chase and to understand his role in the situation," she said. "If you would be more comfortable meeting me with your lawyer present, that would be fine. And if you would rather not come to the detention center, we could meet somewhere else. I am completely at your disposal."

She doubted that the Dobsons would call back. They were influential, and they certainly did not need her. They would gain nothing by contacting her, much less by helping the three unlucky souls who had made the mistake of bringing harm to the heir of this powerful clan.

• • •

For the first twenty minutes of the staff meeting, the youth supervisors reported on how the week had gone, explaining which residents were repeaters and which were new, who was integrating well, who was resisting authority. The youth supervisor in Pod B mentioned Nate Wilson's calm demeanor and politeness, suggesting a future leadership role for him, depending on how long he would remain in detention. In the same breath, he noted Nate's refusal to interact fully with the other residents and wondered if this had to do with his crime or with his personality.

"He talks to me if I initiate conversation," the Pod B supervisor explained, "but he doesn't engage much with the other residents. He doesn't speak up in formal group, but that could change. There's one other boy in the pod who I think he has a lot in common with—Alex Gomez, another first-timer. For one thing, they both read constantly—and the two of them seem to be reading the same books."

"What books?" asked Greta.

"Fantasy. All the Tolkien in the library and several of those big paperbacks with dragons and castles on the covers."

"He's quite advanced," the English teacher reported. "Says he likes Shakespeare. The girl is a fairly advanced reader too—Katie. She hasn't said much in class, but so far she's very solid with the homework."

"What about Renata Le Cortez?" Greta asked.

"She needs to get out of Pod C, people," the art teacher reported sharply. "The girl has been a zombie since day one. She needs to be with *girls*."

"What are the possibilities for moving her?" the social worker asked, glad that someone else had brought this up.

"Zilch at the moment," the assistant superintendent reported glumly.

Renata's pod supervisor concurred. "Believe me, folks, I started pushing for this right away." He added hopefully, "She's a little better since yesterday. She sketches all the time. Seems to prefer being by herself. Draws in her room every chance she gets."

"She's artistic, people," the art teacher announced. "Highly sensitive."

The pod supervisor didn't disagree. "Like I said, she's doing better. Pretty uncommunicative, though. Doesn't talk in formal group. Doesn't talk to anybody most days, including me."

"Isn't there anything we can do about moving her?" the art teacher asked.

"If she'd come in a week earlier, maybe," said the assistant superintendent. "Or if the courts hadn't insisted she be kept separate from the Havenga girl. How is Katie Havenga doing in Pod A?"

"Quite well," her pod supervisor replied. "She hasn't contributed much in group, but she seems to be a careful listener. Rose Lopez has more or less tried to take her under her wing, but Katie is very independent. She journals whenever she's free. Her biggest problem seems to be her mother. The woman works for the Domestic Crisis Center and has taken having a delinquent daughter very hard. She comes every night and basically freaks out in the visiting room."

The assistant superintendent spoke up, addressing Greta, "Has she said anything to you about her mother's visits?"

"Not yet," Greta admitted.

· · ·

When the meeting finally ended, the art teacher, whose name was Andrea, pulled Greta aside and flipped through a short stack of pencil drawings. "Get a load of this."

She lifted an expertly drawn map of North Holmes, signed in one corner with a flourish: *Renata*. "Looks like we have some real talent in our midst."

"She's drawing instead of talking," Greta mused. "Very bridge brain. More typical of boys."

"I know. But she looks thinner every day, Greta. Do you know if she's eating?"

"I'll check."

"Has she seen a psychiatrist?"

"I'm going to try to schedule something, but you know how slammed they are right now," Greta said. "Here's something else that troubles me. No one has come to visit Renata since she was admitted last Monday."

"That's too bad," Andrea said. "She strikes me as a girl who could use some family support."

"She's an only child. I haven't spoken with either parent yet. I hope to very soon. Apparently her mother is an artist."

"Well . . . that explains her talent. What about her father?"

"Some sort of a consultant, I think. Something corporate. I need to know more. Let me know if she says anything interesting to you in class, and I'll keep you posted on getting her relocated."

The social worker breezed through the day area, past the control desk and the other classrooms, down the main hallway, to the security door, where a scanner read the plastic ID she wore around her neck. To her dismay, once settled in her office, the intercom informed her that Claire Havenga had arrived, requesting to see her again.

As Claire approached behind a security guard, the social worker managed a smile and said brightly, "Come in, Claire. Do you mind if I record? I'm still feeling a little groggy with this cold."

"Not at all," Claire insisted. "I do it all the time at the DCC." She smiled, relieved, but then her eyes brimmed. She was already deeply upset.

Date: Friday, June 11
Interview with Claire Havenga
From the videotape:
CH: I remembered something from that Saturday of Memorial Day weekend, while the Dobson boy was at Renata's house . . . against his will, so everyone says. . . .

GS: Excuse me, are you saying you don't believe it, Claire? You don't believe he was there against his will?

CH: The police said they gave him tranquilizers. To keep him quiet. Katie would never do that, Greta. She has never used drugs, never! I'm absolutely sure of that.

GS: There were a lot of drugs in his system. Apparently belonging to the two other mothers. And none of the kids has denied Chase's accusations. If they had—if even one of them had—this would be playing out very differently.

[CH begins to cry.]

GS: I know how upset you are about this, but what were you going to tell me about that Saturday in May? When Chase Dobson was being held in the Cortez home?

CH: How can I be here in this room, talking about my daughter, a girl I would give my life for, a girl who has never been in the slightest bit of trouble. . . .

GS: That Saturday, Claire?

CH: We had a fight. We didn't used to ever fight. But she'd come home from the store with a couple of boxes of cereal, Lucky Charms or something—it's this bright green, fluorescent—God only knows what they put in it and I don't like her to buy that kind of plastic, sugary cereal and I suspected that she had taken money from my purse to buy it with. We were fighting about that, and I must have said something negative about Renata because Katie actually threw the dustpan into a wall and said that I had no right to criticize her perfect friend. She actually called her "my perfect friend." That sneaky little girl.

GS: Why do you say that, Claire? Why do you call Renata "sneaky?"

CH: I don't know. I just could never figure her out. There's something about her, something too polite, or something too . . . I don't know . . . aloof. She wouldn't connect with me. Wouldn't talk to me. But if I ever said anything negative about her, if I uttered the slightest criticism, Katie would just go ballistic.

We'd been fighting more and more. And that Saturday . . . it's just that I was so mad at her . . . for not listening to me about the cereal, and now I know that all the while I was being so mad at her for something so small, she was secretly being an actual criminal! And now I would give anything to just have that girl back, that girl who bought the wrong kind of cereal, but wasn't a criminal. Can you please help me to understand how this could have happened?

[End of videotape]

Saturday, June 11

The social worker had never met Lenora Dobson, but she had seen her in newspaper articles, campaign materials, a United Way calendar. An ad for her real estate company ran frequently on TV. Lenora was a local celebrity, with a polished attractiveness that radiated success.

Lenora had surprised the social worker late Friday afternoon by returning her call and agreeing to meet with her at City Hall the next morning, minus both husband and lawyer.

"I won't discuss Chase's statement," Lenora said. She had a forceful voice, the voice of a woman accustomed to public speaking. "I have no intention of talking about my son without his lawyer present. But I do have insights about the teenagers who victimized him."

"I welcome any information you can give me," the social worker said. "Tomorrow is fine. I am utterly at your disposal, Mrs. Dobson."

"Please," the realtor had insisted, "call me Lenora."

· · ·

In the high-ceilinged conference room at City Hall, the two women were seated on high-backed chairs at either side of one corner of a vast oak table with a glass top and ornately carved legs. Lenora was dressed in a tailored green suit. She was very tan, even for summer, wearing her streaked bleach-blonde hair in a fierce bob.

"My husband doesn't know I'm meeting with you," Lenora announced. Her tone was unapologetic. "Not that he could have changed my mind. I am leaving him out of this because he is still so upset about how the entire case was handled. I'm sure you are aware of the utter incompetence of the North Holmes police. Their efforts to find Chase could be called laughable, if the whole thing hadn't been so unbelievably traumatic for my entire family. And after everything we went through last year with my husband's father. . . ." She shook her head, speechless with aggravation.

"I am so sorry for all that you and your family have been through," the social worker said. "And I know that you and your husband were unhappy with how the case was handled. No one would blame you."

"Complete and utter incompetence at every level," Lenora agreed. "My husband is not yet able to speak calmly about it. And then the business about the school . . . well, the whole thing has made him somewhat unstable. Not that I am not equally upset. I haven't had a normal night of sleep since all of this began."

"How can I help you today, Lenora?" Greta asked.

"I invited you here in order to tell you what I know about the young criminals who kidnapped my son."

"I do welcome anything you can tell me," she said. "May I ask you straightaway if Chase knew any of them personally?"

"Of course he did *not*."

"Are you sure? As I understand it, your son is a well-known athlete with many friends."

"He does have many friends. But those three were not among them. They were not the sort of students that Chase would have had contact with. They are social misfits from dysfunctional families. The boy in particular, the Wilson boy, probably the mastermind—he has a very questionable family situation, which I happen to know about because his mother attends the same church as I do, but surely you already know about his absentee father?"

"I know that James Wilson lives and works in Cleveland. But my understanding is that the Wilsons are not divorced."

"Their so-called 'arrangement' has been going on for years! Those children have not lived with their father for almost two years—can you imagine? The family has been abandoned, no matter how much money he throws at them from wherever he lives now. Sylvia Wilson is completely delusional. The boy probably exists in a chronic state of rage. I wasn't the least surprised when I heard that Sylvia Wilson's boy was one of the three. And then there is the Havenga girl and her awful mother—oh my God—have you met Claire Havenga yet, our local expert on teenage girls?"

"I have," she replied evenly. "How do you two know each other?"

"I worked with her ten years ago when I was on several public school committees, before I was elected to city council. I'll never forget one particular committee—the Teen Pregnancy Task Force—a group of professionals from the community who formed a coalition to advise the schools on the matter of the county's rising pregnancy rate—far above the national average back then, as I recall.

"Claire Havenga had some very strange ideas about what pregnant teenagers need. She joined the committee with a big chip on her shoulder and then cast the dissenting vote on pretty much every decision we made. And she threatened constantly to resign, not that any of us would have minded. Finally, one of the other women asked her pointblank what her problem was, and she informed us loudly that she knew a lot more than any of us about being a pregnant teenager. Apparently, that daughter of hers is the result of a date rape. Claire Havenga was pregnant at *fifteen*."

How many people know this, the social worker wondered. On a small notepad she had brought along with her, she wrote: *Who knows about Katie's father?*

"Claire wanted the last word on teen pregnancy," Lenora continued, "and she certainly got it that day. No one else on the committee had been pregnant at fifteen. But it is really hard for me to imagine her as any sort of reasonable mother, much less a *counselor*! I'm not one bit surprised that daughter of hers is a criminal."

"And the Le Cortez couple," the social worker pressed quietly. "Do you know anything about them?"

"I sold them their *house*!" Lenora exclaimed. "That architectural monstrosity on Dewey Hill—they bought for two million dollars! The wife is an artist, walks with a limp—some sort of terrible car accident back in Charlotte. Whatever sympathy I might have had for her is gone! Those people are the most neglectful, selfish parents you could possibly imagine! And do you know how I know that? Because my son was a prisoner, fighting for his life in their home, the very home that I helped them buy! They were so disconnected from their daughter's life that they never even went down to her bedroom to see how she and her friends were spending their time! They are partly responsible for what my son went through. Right under their noses! They are criminally negligent. *Criminally!*"

She stood up suddenly and leaned over the table, the gold necklace rising and falling against the silk of her blouse. Then she lowered herself back into her chair. The social worker offered to get her a glass of water, an offer the realtor accepted with a wordless nod.

Moments later, as Lenora sipped from a paper cup, the social worker searched for something reassuring to say. "I can't tell you how much I appreciate your willingness to meet with me. You have such a depth of knowledge about this community. And it does seem very odd to me that no one else in the Le Cortez household realized that Chase was being held right there in the house."

"There is a concrete room off the lower level where they kept him," the realtor said flatly; she had completely composed herself. "I can picture it clearly, although it is not pleasant for me to do that now."

The social worker jotted: *must see Cortez home.* Her mind was vibrating with all the new information. "Very good," she said. "May I call you if I have other questions?"

"You have my phone numbers," the realtor said. "But I must warn you, I'm going to be hard to reach for the next few weeks, very busy with lawyers and such."

. . .

On the drive home, the social worker recalled that she knew the junior high soccer and tennis coach, the man who would have been dealing directly with Chase on a regular basis. She had met him the summer before; he was married to one of the court recorders. She even recalled his name—Martin Collier. Perhaps he would talk to her about Chase. She would call him first thing Monday.

First GreyMount Katie

I can see her, Journal, clear as yesterday. It was back in April, a Saturday like today—my favorite day of the week, until I got locked up in here. Renata is sitting in the blue puffy chair in her fantastic bedroom, and she is sinking deeper and deeper into the chair. She has something to tell me, something she has been trying to tell me for weeks and something she is afraid to tell me. Whatever it is, it's making her sink down and look really scared. I am scared too, because I noticed for the past few weeks that something is bothering her; she has been really nervous and quiet and sad. I thought it might have something to do with Nate, and so I was also afraid that what she was about to tell me would make me sad too, and I try really hard never to get sad about anything so that I don't get so sad that I can never be happy again.

But it wasn't about Nate.

This was what Renata said: "Something awful is happening to me, Katie."

I had a terrible thought—a thought that she might be sick or dying. But when I asked her if she was sick, she shook her head, and I was so relieved.

But then more tears came. Coming from her brown eyes and splashing off her black eyelashes and bouncing down to the front of her yellow shirt. I remembetr that shirt, my favorite of all her amazing clothes. I asked her to please tell me exactly what was happening.

> *Renata: Some boys at your school are following me. Making fun of me. My name and my hair and my size.*

Was she shrinking before my eyes? Was the chair growing? She told me about those boys in the hall. She didn't know who they were, but I knew. I knew which boys she meant without her even having to tell me.

> *Me: Tell me what they do.*

> *Renata: When they see me in the hall, they make a circle around me. Five or six boys and their leader. The leader is really tall with a horrible cruel face and he is always there, but sometimes the*

> *others change. They call him Dobson. I try not*
> *to look at him because it's so much worse if I look*
> *at him; it's like he gets even meaner and louder*
> *and more terrible if I look at him.*

She had started to cry again. But I was turning to steel inside.

Me: What does he do when you come closer?

Renata: [Crying] He calls me a boy. He asks me why
I'm wearing chick clothes if I'm a guy. He asks if
I'm a fag. He says it really loud. Everyone hears.
No one helps me. Do you think I look like a boy,
Katie?

Me: Oh God, no.

Renata: Then why does he say that? He calls me Rico.
Like with a fake Spanish accent. And he says I'm
pretending to be a girl. He says . . . he says I'm
hiding my dick. And then they all laugh their
evil laughs. Why? Why is that funny?

Me: It's not funny. And you don't look like a boy, Renata.
You're just . . . small. Small and perfect.

Renata: They laugh and laugh and it gets louder and
scarier and they follow me. It's like they'll never
stop laughing at me. Am I ugly? Is that the
reason?

Me: There isn't a reason. You're the victim of the week, that's all.

Renata: It's been going on for more than a week. Three whole weeks. Almost an entire month. Ever since spring break.

Me: Why didn't you tell me about it sooner?

Renata: I was so embarrassed. And I thought it would stop. I thought they would get tired of tormenting me if I didn't fight back. But it's just getting worse. Today was so horrible. The leader started walking behind me, crouching down to make himself smaller and making fun of how I walk. He followed me like that all the way to my biology class. I think I might have to stop going to school, Katie.

Me: Don't say that! I would die without you at school! I'll find a way to protect you. We have to talk to Nate.

Renata: Please don't tell Nate! I don't want him to see me this way. A person that other boys mock and torment.

So I told her about us getting stung. How it happened before we met her. How our friends turned on us. And that I had never told her about it because I didn't want her to see me that way either. And I told her the names of the kids who had been our friends but who weren't our friends anymore. Some of them she knew; some she didn't know, but she listened and it stopped her tears. I told her about that month before she came to North Holmes. How we felt like outcasts every day.

And while I was telling her this, Journal, she closed her eyes and shivered and hugged herself.

Renata: What a dark and terrible place your school is.

Me: I know. We have to tell Nate. He's a guy. He understands guys better than we do. We'll ask him what we should do to make them stop.

Renata: Okay. Thank you. I'm glad I told you. I was afraid to tell you.

Then she just fell asleep in her chair. I think she was just so tired from holding in all that pain. I went over to the chair and woke her up just a little, and I helped her take the few steps to her bed with its leather headboard and blue puffy bedspread and six pillows. She fell backward against the blue pillows and was soon asleep again. It reminded me of a little girl, the way she was sleeping, on her back with her arms up near her head, so small and sad with the tears still wet on her cheeks.

• • •

I rode my bike to Nate's. He lives in a subdivision, nicer than my neighborhood, with more expensive houses and better lawns. Although now his house is kind of a mess.

Nate says it was the nicest house on the block before his dad took that job in Cleveland, but in the last few years, it's gotten really run-down.

Nate lives in a room in the basement that was once his father's workshop which he says it is better than having to share a room with his brothers. He came to the door and saw it was me.

> *Nate: Let's get out of here, Katie. Sylvia is a lunatic today.*

Sylvia is pretty much always a lunatic. She's always making fun of because they're so stupid. Like no talking in the living room from 3:00 to 5:00 because that's Sylvia's naptime and her bedroom is next to the living room.

> *Nate: She's announced that I'm not allowed ever to enter her bedroom or her bathroom. She thinks I'm going to steal her prescription drugs; she saw something about it on television. God, if I was going to steal anything from her, it would be money for a decent meal once in a while. Get me out of here, okay?*

Before we left, Nate's sister Natalie came into the living room and saw me at the door, but she didn't say hello. She doesn't like me. She is Nate's exact polar opposite, I swear. She is so stuck up. Nate doesn't like to talk about her, so I don't ask. We rode our bikes to the downtown café and went inside to sit at our favorite booth, the one right at the window. Then I told him what those boys at school were doing to Renata. Especially their leader. How he calls her Rico. How he asks her really loud why she dresses like a girl if she's a boy. How he makes fun of her walk. And that really mean remark about her having a dick. When I told him that part he put his hands over his eyes and groaned.

Nate: Oh, shit. Oh shit, oh shit. It's Chase Dobson, isn't it?

Me: How do you know that? Did Renata already tell you?

Nate: I just know it's him.

Me: Well, you're right. Renata was hoping he would get tired of harassing her and then the other boys would stop and leave her alone.

Nate: It won't stop. I guarantee it won't stop.

Me: Wait a minute . . . how do you know it won't stop? Seriously, Nate, how did you know it was Chase and how do you know it won't stop?

Nate: He's doing it because of me, Katie. He knows she's my friend.

Me: Why would he care if Renata is your friend?

Nate: He's just . . . he's trying to get back at me.

Me: Get back at you? What would Chase Dobson have to get back at you for?

Nate: Well . . . I helped him once. Last year.

*Me: Helped him? Why would you help him? He's like one
of the most horrible boys at our school!*

Nate covered his ears. I pulled one of his hands away
from his ears so that he had to hear me.

Me: Nate!

*Nate: I know, I know, he's really messed-up, Katie. I
know that. And now he's trying to hurt me by
hurting Renata.*

I looked across the table at Nate and just stared into his
eyes, waiting for more explanation. Nate has the purest,
cleanest blue eyes

*Nate: Look, I'll tell you everything, just not now. Right
now we have to help Renata. She's caught in the
middle. We have to stop Chase. We have to show
him that he can't get away with this!*

Right then another question came flying into my head,
and I just had to ask.

Me: Nate, are you and Renata hooking up?

Because I was suddenly feeling like there were too
many things I didn't know. Like I didn't know Renata was
being persecuted by Chase because of Nate, for example.
I didn't even know that Nate *knew* Chase. I didn't know

that Nate once helped Chase. So all of a sudden it seemed possible that Nate and Renata could be hooking up. I was still staring into his blue eyes, holding my coffee real tight and staring, holding my breath, bracing for how much it was going to hurt me if he said that the answer was yes.

But his expression changed and got really, really kind.

Nate: Katie. Katie. Renata's not my girlfriend.

I was so relieved, I could have cried. We were all still best friends, nothing had changed. But I told him right there that if something like that ever did happen, if he ever did get feelings like that about Renata, he had to tell me because I've been his friend the longest.

Nate: You're not just my friend, Katie. You're my GreyMount. My true sister.

He lifted up my hand to his mouth and kissed it. Not like a romantic thing because we aren't like that. More like something a prince would do. It almost makes me want to cry, remembering that moment. How close I felt to him. How I would do anything for him. How deep and pure our friendship was that day.

I have to stop. It's almost time for them to take my pen away and I can't let Lee Ann or Rosie or anybody in Pod A see me cry.

 nathaniel, Son of James

Journal
Day Six of Captivity

Noonday: Long before I joined with my first GreyMount, in the early days of my Year of Watchfulness, my trial began with words, Great She. Four words, to be exact. Spoken by me with urgency and compassion in a small, windowless room. Four words that released a waterfall of words. A confession. One hour of one night that pulled me from my own despair into a time of hope, followed quickly by more silence and distance. Do you understand? I was pulled in, Great She. I would not have dared approach him. The Master of Contortions reached out to me. I would never have sought his company because I am

Nathaniel, I am different. I'm a warrior of words, rather than weapons and battles, and I don't have anything he needs. Or so I thought.

The night of our first meeting was in August, the final week, an aimless summer during which I had lived in confusion and sorrow at The Great Departure of James of Cleves. All during those sad days I took lessons from a guardian who admired my writing earlier in the year and this guardian had mentored me during the summer months in the telling of my tales. I met this guardian at the Great Hall, but often, except for us, the hall was empty. That night I had finished my hour of consultation, and my mentor had departed. I was leaving through a doorway at the back of the building, near the game and battalion area, where there is an exit close to the Arena of Champions, through the Training Chambers and the Rooms of Fortification. As I passed through these spaces, I heard the sound of weeping—sobbing, Great She! And lo! in a small room, I found a warrior, crouched and leaning against a cabinet, having collapsed onto the floor.

Another time, I would have left him to his private tears, but on that night I felt unusually brave and compassionate, having myself recently been reduced many times to solitary tears, thinking about The Great Departure and missing my father. So I stayed in the doorway. He kept his face turned to the wall, until I spoke the four fateful words. I asked only: Who has hurt you?

And the warrior turned to me and although his fore-locks nearly covered his face, I saw that it was the Master of Contortions and that his tears were real. And he told me that he wept not because he had been hurt but because of one whom he had himself hurt. I asked him who that was. And he told me, Great She. He told me his story. I knelt before him and offered him my own story, which he accepted, shedding many more tears against my worn and faded shirt. Afterward he thanked me, begging me to tell no one of our conversation, and I promised him, on my honor. I swore that I would not.

Perhaps on that night he also meant to honor our secret. But I know that he came to regret that he had told me. He became afraid of what I knew and unhappy that I had seen him in a state of brokenness. Eventually, I realized that my compassion had put me in great danger. But I never thought I would end up in the Place of Contrition, at the mercy of my captors, alone, cut off from my sisters, apart from them, as I have lived so long apart from the only other person in the world who might have helped me.

On that summer night, I saw the Master of Contortions in a light that no one else had ever seen him in—not his clan, not his guards, not any of his maidens, I am sure of this. Not his mother, who binds his wounds after each competition, nor his father, who counsels him tirelessly in matters of conquest, nor his grandfather, who comes unbidden into his dreams, and torments him from the grave.

Do you believe me, Great She, when I tell you that I saw the Master's tears? That his tears mingled with my own tears? I had no fear that night. And this was a grave mistake, Great She—to comfort the Master without fear. But on that night, during that hour, I did not know. Only much later did I know. Then for many months I escaped the Master's gaze by slipping back into the shadows, disappearing into the invisibility of my station. I made sure that for weeks, months, almost an entire year, the Master did not see me and I did not see him. I hoped that he would forget me, though I could not forget him, nor the things that he had told me in his hour of confession. And I thought that he truly had forgotten me, Great She, but all the same, I prepared myself and kept my GreyMount close, preparing her and tightening the bonds that connected me with her.

But the Master was also preparing. He waited for a long time, months, long enough for me to believe that no harm would come to me, but in the springtime of this year, he sought out my second GreyMount, my newer, smaller sister, and thus did he force my hand by bringing her most cruelly to public disgrace and anguish.

Now, though I am the imprisoned one, while the Master walks freely in the village, I am victorious because I did not falter in my efforts to rescue my smaller sister. The truth of this sustains me every day and every hour.

Now I walk from my Pod of Brothers into the Common Room, to the Rooms of Instruction and the Place of Games, and back to the Pod of Brothers, where daily I must engage with my fellow prisoners. I am ever impatient to be left alone to write as I am born to this task, to fade into my private cell where only my thoughts, my memories of the one who is far from me, and my beloved Tolkien can bring solace.

There is one other prisoner who shares my love for J. R. R., the trilogy passes back and forth between us like a Holy Ark. I see him reading the book I have just finished in the Common Room; he reads with a hunger I know well. He is Alex, and he is small of stature and dark-eyed and watchful. During the Time of Forced Confessions, he sometimes turns his gaze to me, as though encouraging me to speak.

But I do not speak.

What is his crime, Great She? Why does he dwell in the Place of Contrition? Can you tell me? I do not feel free to ask him directly since I cannot reciprocate and reveal the twisted path that has led me to be imprisoned with him.

The days are long, Great She, the sky darkens late; sometimes there is a glimmer of light in the high windows over my cot before I sleep. This light also consoles me and guides me into my dreams as darkness falls. I am locked into the room until morning, but this I do not mind—for I feel most alive and free within the tiny space. There is a window on the door to my room with a shade that can be lifted, but no one lifts it, and so far the other prisoners leave me alone and give me my privacy, because I am Nathaniel, Chief GreyMount, scribe and messenger. I am not afraid and not ashamed, even though I am in exile, even as I walk through the Place of Contrition, I am not quite here; I am partly not here, as a person in a dream.

First GreyMount Katie

Journal Entry Monday, June 13—After Lunch Break

Oh man. An hour ago, Mrs. Shield pulled me out of English and brought me into this little private room off the multi-purpose room and asked me if I'm doing okay.

I like Mrs. Shield, Journal. I like that she doesn't seem upset or shocked that I'm actually in juvie. She acts almost like it's normal for a kid to be in here. She doesn't treat me like a criminal, she just talks to me really straight, no feeling sorry for me, no tears. And whenever she's done talking to me, she always says, "Later, Katie," and she does this thing with her face—scrunching it, like a smile is forcing itself out through her sadness. And then her whole face shines for just a second. I guess you could call it a pretty smile. But most of the time, she just looks extremely tired. And she blows her nose quite a lot so it's always very red and sore.

She asked me if there was anything I need to talk about. Like anything weighing heavily on my mind since our first meeting.

And so I told her that Renata is weighing heavily on my mind because I don't see how she can stand it in here, especially since I heard from Lee Ann that they put her in a pod with boys! I can't believe that they would do that to her after what happened to her at school! And the boys in Pod C are like little miniature criminals! I almost wanted to cry when I heard this. So I asked Mrs. Shield if she thought it was a good idea for Renata to be in a pod with boys. I asked her really politely. And Mrs. Shield put one hand on her forehead and shook her head, like she knew this was a major screw-up and she was really sorry.

Mrs. Shield: I have spoken with several people about that very issue and we are trying to make some other arrangement for Renata.

Me: When did you talk to her?

Mrs. Shield: I met with her a few days ago.

Me: When will you talk to her again?

Mrs. Shield: Today.

Me: Because I think you should probably talk to her every

single day to make sure she isn't losing it. Especially being surrounded by boys.

Mrs. Shield: Trust me, I am keeping careful track of both your friends, Katie. The main thing now is for you to concentrate on your own situation and keep writing in your journal. Are you sure there isn't anything else you want to talk to me about? Are you doing okay with your mother's visits? I know she has been coming to see you every day. How has that been for you?

She asked me this like she knew something about my mom. It made me nervous.

Me: Have you met her?

Mrs. Shield. Yes, I have.

Which made me even more nervous!

There is no telling what my mom will tell Mrs. Shield. Even though she doesn't know what really happened, she might say some off-the-wall stuff about Renata, who I am pretty sure she blames for this whole mess, which is just so unfair and blind. This is what I said to Mrs. Shield:

Me: I wish she wasn't visiting me every single day, if you want the truth.

Mrs. Shield: She's worried about you, Katie. I don't think she ever expected you to get into such serious trouble. My impression is that she has always thought you were a perfect daughter and that the two of you were very close, almost like sisters. Feel free to write about your mother in your journal if it would help you. Anything you want to put into words.

And while she was saying this, I was thinking: I've already put stuff about my mother into words, Mrs. Shield. Too bad I can't let you read it.

Journal Entry Tuesday, June 14—After Lunch Break

Big fight in the visiting room with Guess Who last night. She came to tell me that she's figured out that what we did to Chase Dobson was on account of she hasn't been spending enough time with me! She asked me if "acting out" was my way to get back at her for not being a stay-at-home mom! I am not exaggerating—this is what I deal with all the time.

I lost it, Journal. I snapped. I put my hands on the sides of my head and I screamed at her: "MOM! WHY DOES EVERY SINGLE THING THAT HAPPENS TO ME HAVE TO BE ABOUT YOU?"

She was sitting across the table from me in the visitation room and everybody stopped and looked at us, and then Mom pushed her chair away from the table, put her head down almost to her knees and started to cry—and I mean CRY—so loud everybody back in my pod probably heard it. I begged her to stop. I reached across the table to make up with her, and then she just jumped on me and wrapped her arms around my shoulders really tight and gave me this insanely tight hug. Seriously I almost wanted to call a guard to get her off me.

> Mom: Haven't I always been the kind of mom you could tell anything to? Haven't I? Why are you being so cold to me? Why are you shutting me out? Don't you see how much I want to help you! Don't you understand where you are?

> Me: Mom, please, it's not so bad, I'm doing okay. I'm handling it pretty well, everybody says so, even my social worker. I really need you to stop crying every time you come to see me.

> Mom: Then tell me this, Miss Hardened Criminal. Didn't you even once consider that plotting revenge with your friends might get you stuck in goddamn juvenile detention?

And the truth was, Journal, her question stopped me, because there was this moment, this moment after Chase had been at Renata's for five nights and he was in his room with the door closed, and Renata was sitting in her little private kitchen, and she was pouring the Lucky Charms into a bowl for him, and she looked over the counter and caught me staring at her and getting upset.

Renata: Please don't look at me like that, Katie. He's leaving soon. He promised. And he promised that none of us will get into trouble.

Me: Why do you believe him? Why do you even talk to him? Why are you bringing him cereal? Don't you understand, Renata? You can't trust him. You can't trust what he says.

Renata: We had a really good talk today. And he said he would make up a story for his parents so that none of us will get blamed. I do believe him, Katie. He's sorry for what he did to me. And he's had a really hard life, same as you, same as me.

Me: Jesus, he's not like us, Renata! He's a bully! He's a liar! He's lying to you now so you'll feel sorry for him. He doesn't care if we get in trouble. He doesn't care about any of us. Not even Nate. Don't forget who he is, Renata. Don't forget how all this started.

I remembered those words, while my mom was sobbing in the Visitor's Room.

Mom: Please, big girl. Answer me. Didn't you know you would wind up in here for what you did?

Me: Maybe I sort of knew at the end.

Mom: At the END? You didn't know at the BEGINNING? What in God's name were you

THINKING at the BEGINNING? Kidnapping a boy who comes from one of the most powerful families in this town—his grandfather was the MAYOR, for God's sake—giving him pills and keeping him a prisoner and not telling anyone— this felt like something you should TRY?

And then I just so much wanted to tell her the truth, Journal. I wanted to stop being First GreyMount Katie and tell her everything. Including the things that happened that we never planned. Including the things that we promised never to reveal. Including the terrible thing I learned from Chase about her. I wanted to just throw myself against her and cry and sob and beg her to take me home, like I was nine years old and I still believed that she knew everything and she could fix anything, and it was fine that it was just the two of us and all we needed was each other and nothing this bad could ever happen.

But I wouldn't have been able to tell her everything. Because I don't know everything. I think there are some really, really important things that I don't know. Things Nate knows, or maybe Renata knows, or maybe even Chase knows, but I don't know. The more I write about what happened, the more I realize all the things I don't know. Because there is a secret story and it is inside of another secret story and that one is inside of another secret story. We all promised that we wouldn't tell the whole story, but Journal, there are so many stories that I don't know which one is which anymore.

So last night Mom finally leaves, not crying anymore, but still acting all hurt and confused. I will be nicer to her when she comes back, which will probably be tomorrow night—way too soon. In the meantime, I have to figure out what I'm going to do about all this writing and writing that nobody but me can read.

Journal Entry Tuesday, June 14—Evening Personal Time

Okay, seriously, you will not BELIEVE what I found today in the classroom that is for my English Lit class. Inside a cupboard where the English teacher told us to put our homework when it was done was a stack of empty journals just like the one Mrs. Shield gave me one week ago. Exactly the same. Why were they there? I don't know. But Journal, I am saved.

Katie Havenga's Journal for Mrs. Shield

Hi my name is Katie Havenga, and this is my journal, and I have been in the Ferndale Juvenile Detention Center since ten days ago when I first got arrested for something that me and my friends did to a boy at my school named Chase Dobson. Basically we kidnapped Chase because of what he was doing to my friend Renata and because somebody had to stop him because he is one of those boys who thinks nobody can stop him from doing anything he wants to do, and he probably still thinks that—I really don't know, I hope I never see him again. At least while I'm in here, I know I won't have to see him. That is one good thing about being in detention.

Here I am in Pod A and the other girls in my pod are: Rhonda, Julia, Sam, Rosario, Kathy, Janie, and

Renee—eight girls including me. I guess they call it a pod because we are like the peas that are separated from other peas in the other pods or whatever. My best friends Renata and Nate are in different pods, so I don't see them or get to ever talk to them, and I was not expecting this. I thought we would all be together in here, and it wouldn't be so bad, just like school wasn't so bad as long as we were dealing with stuff all together, and we could laugh about it, walking to my house after school or going for coffee or going over to Renata's house and hanging out there.

The person that I talk to the most in my pod is Rosie, but I don't really talk very much to anybody because I miss my friends so much and because I am basically just trying to get through this, and I don't want any more drama in my life because I have enough of that from my mom who is majorly freaked out that I am in juvie, and she comes to see me like every night and breaks down and cries at least once. Sometimes I kind of wish that the staff would not let her in. I guess I could refuse to go to the Visitor's Room, but I think that it would kill her if she couldn't come here and see me, and if I did that her death would be my fault and then I would feel even more guilty than I already feel about everything. So I just sit down with her and wait for her tears. I try to tell her that I am okay and she doesn't have to cry about me, but every once in a while I lose my temper and say something that makes her feel worse and then I am always sorry. She has a very stressful job at the Domestic Crisis Center, but since I've been in here she is more stressed out than I have ever seen her, and honestly, I'm a little worried about her, in case I find out I have to stay in here longer and then I don't know if she'll be able to handle it. What would she do? Probably move in here with me; she could take Rosie's room, she said she is going home in a week. She said she doesn't want to go home, she doesn't mind being here. She said it's better for her to just stay in juvie, that's how insane her mom and her stepdad are. It's pretty hard for me to imagine not wanting to get out of this place, but I guess for some kids, it's an improvement over their normal life.

Everybody is basically being nice to me and I think I'm doing okay. Well, actually the first day was pretty bad and finding out that I wasn't going to get to see Nate and Renata was hard, and turning in my clothes was horrible and hearing that noise that the big metal doors make when you go inside the prison part, and then sleeping in my room after they locked me in was pretty bad, but I thought about how much I love my friends and how I would do anything for them, and that comforted me. And the next morning, our youth specialist, her name is Lee Ann, she introduced me to the other girls and they all said hello to me. Lee Ann seems very friendly and fair. My teachers seem nice, nicer than most of the teachers at school. Especially the art teacher—she's very nice. My caseworker is nice—his name is Mark. Mrs. Shield, you are nice. I haven't talked to the guy who is going to be my lawyer yet, my mom said she sort of knows him, I hope he will also be nice, and I hope that he can get us out of here.

In my pod, our color is blue and so we all wear blue shirts and blue pants and blue sweatshirts and they make us wear slippers unless we are going to the gym or going outside. It's like we are all wearing pajamas all the time. Some of the girls hate the sweats and they hate the underwear because it's faded and worn out because it's been washed a million times and it's ugly, but those are not the kind of things that bother me so much. I am not what you'd call a clothes person, and I don't really care what I look like while I am in here. When I first came in, I had to take out my earrings and take off my one ring. That seemed strange, to have to do that—like did they think I was going to stab somebody with my ear stud? Rosie and Janie say they miss their boyfriends all the time, but I don't have a boyfriend, and I don't think about boys so much. I have learned that if you don't pay any attention to boys, if you don't look at them or talk to them, after a while you start to become invisible and that works better for me. Boys ignore me, and it's better. Maybe that is why nothing like what happened to Renata has ever happened to me. Renata is one of those girls who really stands out in a crowd. She knows she is different and doesn't try to hide her different-ness even though she is shy. She is brave that way. Also she doesn't flirt with boys, she is just purely herself. The reason those boys went after her is because of Nate. Something about Nate and Chase. I don't know exactly what it was, something old. Maybe I'm wrong about this. Forget I said that.

Right now I am sitting by myself in my little cell in Pod A. Before I came here, I always pictured that there would be a bunch of kids in a cell with me and we'd be sleeping on bunk beds like in the movies but it isn't like that at all. I sleep in this tiny little cement room, and I have this bed that is like a cot that comes out from the wall. I have a sheet, an itchy blanket, and a really flat pillow (like cardboard). It's not that comfortable, but I sleep okay most of the time. A couple of the first nights I had nightmares but I think it was just because I couldn't get used to the idea that I was stuck in here and couldn't go home.

I have a little desk in my room, and there is a little toilet and a sink, and I have this little cupboard for my hygiene kit stuff which is a hairbrush, soap, deodorant (it doesn't work), a toothbrush, and toothpaste. That's it, Journal. My face is dry as a paper towel, and my hair looks terrible every day, but so does everybody else's. We exercise in the gym, and I kind of like that, and I feel like my arms and legs are getting stronger than when I first came here. There is no television-watching. There are no computers that we can use. There are books, lots of books. Right now I am reading *A Tree Grows in Brooklyn*. It's ancient, but so far, it's pretty good.

Sometimes when I am in bed I think about Renata sleeping in the same kind of bed that I am sleeping in. I know that she probably has insomnia. She has the coolest bedroom ever—with a huge bed and tons of pillows and the world's softest mattress that you sink down in like a cloud. Plus all her sheets and blankets are new. A few times I slept over at her house on her bed, and it was like I was sleeping in a hotel, which is something I have never done. I think about Renata sleeping on a cot that comes right out of the wall and having a scratchy blanket and it really hurts me, it hurts me. I don't know what she's thinking and before I came in here, I knew what she was thinking every day. We talked about everything. Every single day.

It's time for gym. I can't wait to go outside. The sky is really blue today. I can see the sky through the little windows. Rosie and I are going to run laps. She said she wants to lose five pounds before she goes home, but I just want to run. When I run I can pretend that I can run anywhere, anywhere I want under the sky and there's not a tall fence around the playground and I can walk home when I'm done and I'm not stuck in here, I'm not in juvie at all.

Social Worker

Wednesday, June 15

Her first call of the day was from Claire, something that didn't surprise her; she had heard about the latest mother-daughter meltdown in the Visitor's Room from the night staffer:

> *Katie came back to pod Monday night obviously upset. She didn't talk to any of the other girls for the rest of the evening, and seems very unhappy today. I was just starting to feel like she was making progress socially. Somebody needs to tell Supermom to stop coming around every day and give the poor girl a chance to make something positive of her time in here.*

"How are you this morning, Claire?"

"I was up all night," Claire replied. "I'm so worried about Katie."

"Katie is fine," the social worker insisted. "I'm planning to meet with her just as soon as—"

"She is not fine," Claire interrupted. "I don't know what she is, but she's not fine. It's like she's frozen—something has hardened inside of her. And I can't help but think that it has something to do with Renata. Like she has some kind of—I don't know—*power* over my daughter. I was up all night, thinking about this. And I started having memories about last spring and how different Katie seemed, even before all this business started. Even before they did such an awful thing. Something changed her, Greta. Something came between us and made her shut me out."

"Say more about that," the social worker prompted. "Say more about Katie and Renata. You mentioned before that you did not have a good feeling about their friendship."

"After Katie met Renata, she started saying that she had two best friends. Before that, it was Nate, only Nate. And I adore Nate, as you know, he's the sweetest boy in the world—I can't believe he got himself into this terrible mess! But Renata . . . there was just something about her, Greta. It was like she didn't trust me. She wouldn't look at me, and she was too quiet around me, and the few times she did talk, she was too polite. She seemed phony. I tried to talk to her, but then I started to ignore just her because I couldn't read her. She was just . . . secretive. That's the word that comes to me. Deliberately secretive."

While Claire spoke, the social worker wrote on a notepad: *Secretive?* Aloud she said, "I plan to meet with each of them tomorrow, after I've read their journals. Why don't I give you a call at the end of the day tomorrow?"

Claire agreed and left. Inspired by her success, the social worker called the Le Cortez household again; no one had yet responded to her two earlier messages. This time a woman answered, speaking in a sonorous voice with a slight accent.

"Is there something I can help you with, Mrs. Shield?" she asked.

"I've been thinking that I might have a better awareness of what transpired between your daughter and her friends if I could see the exact area in your house that Chase Dobson was . . . confined in."

"Of course you can see it," the artist agreed, impatiently, as though she had hoped for a more significant request. "You may stop by this afternoon if that would be convenient for you."

Pressing her luck, the social worker dialed Nate Wilson's home phone number. Her earlier calls had been answered by an answering machine with a generic male voice. She'd left two very clear, open-ended messages, inviting someone from the household to contact her. She had also carefully recited the visiting hours at the

JDC—every evening at 7:00 P.M. and Saturday and Sunday afternoons from 12:00 to 3:00.

This time a person answered—a distinctly young and female person. The school day had started an hour ago, but the bright "Hello" clearly belonged to a teenager.

"Yes, this is Greta Shield calling from the Juvenile Detention Center. May I speak with Sylvia Wilson please?"

A slight pause. "You mean . . . about my brother?"

"Is your mother there?"

"Are you from the juvie place?"

"I'm your brother's social worker. Is your mother home?"

The voice took on a more measured authority. "My mom doesn't want to talk to anybody from juvie," the girl announced. "She told me no exceptions."

"Would it be possible for me to—"

"She is not available." The girl hung up.

. . .

Magdalena Le Cortez answered the doorbell at the mansion's front door, wearing a puffy artist smock over black leggings. The smock hid her torso, but revealed thin arms and legs and a glamorously long neck. She wore her hair in a black twist at the back of her head, the spiral held fast with an ivory comb. Silver jewelry in bold shapes decorated both wrists and many fingers. She was leaning on a wooden cane, the handle carved in the shape of a crane.

"I am alone today," the artist told the social worker. "My husband left early this morning for Charlotte." She smiled—red lips, perfect teeth, a slight sideways tilt of the head.

The social worker followed her into a large foyer, noticing her hostess's pronounced limp. From the foyer, the artist led her guest to a carpeted stairway descending to the lower level. "I assume you will also want to see Renata's bedroom? I must ask you to proceed without me. I'm afraid the legs are not good today. I will be in my studio, and we can speak afterward."

The social worker hurried down the stairs, thrilled to be able to privately inspect Renata's bedroom and the scene of the kidnapping. At the bottom of the stairs, French doors opened into an apartment with its own kitchen, bath, sitting area, and one large bedroom. There was a separate entrance off the sitting room, a heavy door leading to the Le Cortez garage. She stood in the center of the sitting room. The space appeared to have been professionally cleaned; it smelled of furniture polish, window spray, and air freshener.

Renata's adjacent bedroom was large enough for both a king-sized bed with a tall leather headboard and a vast picture window providing a view of Lake Michigan. There were two large paintings on the walls, both signed *MAGDALENA*, in curling black scrawl.

The social worker next poked her head into a walk-in closet and saw that Renata Le Cortez had filled the shelves of the closet with art supplies, sketch pads and unfinished art projects. There was an easel against the far wall with several empty canvases. Closer to the door was a small section of Renata's actual clothing, mostly jeans and T-shirts in neat stacks. The room was probably bigger than Renata's cell at the JDC.

She proceeded to the "laundry room," and looked around, surprised that the police had described the room this way; she would have called it something very different—a kind of personal recreation room, significantly less deluxe than anything else she had glimpsed inside the house, but still spacious, comfortable, and clean—with a futon against one wall, a small dresser in one corner, an old reclining chair in front of a TV, small refrigerator, treadmill, and weight bench. A wooden card table with four chairs sat near the bed. In the farthest corner were a washer and dryer. Above these appliances were two egress windows that the social worker was able to easily push outward. The windows led to a deep ravine behind the house. They were small openings, but not too small for a teenager to crawl through, if he was determined to escape.

There were three other closed doors in the laundry room and the social worker opened each of them—two closets and a utilitarian bathroom with toilet, sink, and shower.

Greta sat down on the edge of the cot and studied the room, the place where Chase had spent six days in May. He would have been alone for three days while his captors were attending school—with access to an obvious exit, if he were locked in.

What did he do during those days? Renata herself would have had the most frequent and intimate contact with him—the same girl he had tormented publicly before he became her prisoner. His prison and her bedroom were separated by only a wall. It didn't make sense. Why would Renata have accepted this arrangement? How had she endured it for so many days?

. . .

Magdalena was in her studio—a vast, high-ceilinged room on the other side of the house's midsection. Windows dominated the walls, but each of the room's four corners were piled with canvases, used and unused, and there were a dozen or more paintings against one interior wall. These appeared to be part of an animal series, large paintings in bold colors—deer, wolves, fish, owls, moths, and turtles. The social worker saw that each animal had some sort of human quality—the owl had a human face, the turtles had hands and feet, the moths had human bodies. The artist was seated on a stool at her easel, dabbing at a painting of a girl clinging to the back of a crow.

Magdalena half-turned, paintbrush in the air, and observed her guest. Her smile was unreadable. The social worker thought: *she knows I don't know what to make of this studio, this art, this information.*

After a silent moment, Magdalena asked, "Would you care for coffee, Mrs. Shield?"

She said yes, hoping that this meant that Magdalena would be willing to converse about her daughter. The artist put down her paintbrush and limped over to a free-standing marble-topped counter with a small stereo, a closed laptop, and an espresso machine. "Did you find what you were looking for?" she asked.

"I wasn't looking for anything in particular," the social worker replied. "Just . . . hoping to get a sense of what one week in your laundry room would have been like for a boy like Chase Dobson."

"*My* laundry room is on this level," the artist corrected. "Renata does her own laundry. That is one of many reasons why I have no need to go downstairs."

"I see. And the fitness equipment—your husband's?"

"Some. A few items for my own rehabilitation. Which I use less and less often now that I'm painting again. This is my rehabilitation, you see." She waved around the room, her face softening into a bright, unaffected smile. The social worker felt a pang of confusion. Why hadn't this woman expressed the slightest concern about her daughter?

Magdalena set a cup of espresso on a small table near where Greta was standing. Greta thanked her hostess; the coffee was devastatingly strong and it focused her. "Are you worried about Renata, Mrs. Cortez?" she asked.

"Not at all," the artist replied calmly. "She is in a safe place. She can be alone. She must contemplate the consequences of her actions. Her father and I will see to whatever needs to be done in order to move her forward in her life. I myself was in trouble quite frequently as a teenager, Mrs. Shield. I haven't forgotten what those years were like. They fuel my art, even today."

"I don't imagine you kidnapped anyone."

Magdalena turned back to the canvas and picked up her brush. She touched the canvas lightly—a few strands of gold in the girl's brown hair. "It was a highly original form of rebellion. But it will all be resolved before summer's end."

"Were you surprised that Renata did not come to you for help, Mrs. Le Cortez? I mean with what was happening to her at the school?"

The artist continued painting. "Do you have children, Mrs. Shield?" she asked.

The social worker stiffened. "No," she said. "But I work with young people every day."

"Of course. That is your profession. Perhaps you are one of those adults who thinks it odd when teenagers don't tell their parents everything?"

The social worker waited.

The artist went on. "I happen to think it is perfectly normal for teenagers to guard their secrets carefully. Renata is a proud girl from a proud family. I have no trouble understanding why she didn't tell me that she was being persecuted in her new world."

The social worker took another bracing sip of espresso. "I expect you have been asked this many times, but I can't help wondering if you ever heard any suspicious or unfamiliar noises coming from below?"

"If you were to take this powerful little stereo down to the room below and play it at full volume, then come back to where you are standing now, I guarantee, you would hear nothing. It's an old house, very thick walls and floors, unlike the houses of today. But if I might point out something else . . . your question assumes that the person in the room below us was crying out for help. Might you be mistaken in this assumption? Perhaps there were reasons why this boy was not crying out for help at all."

"Are you referring to the drugs that were found in his system?"

Magdalena shrugged. "That is the easiest explanation, I suppose."

"What are you suggesting?"

"As I said, children have secrets. All children. Family secrets. Secrets of identity. Secret desires and abilities. It is one of the ways that we survive the families we are born into. My daughter has a secret. And perhaps the boy who preferred to be missing for a while also has a secret. A reason for hiding that no one has yet uncovered."

"You seem to have thought about this quite a bit, Mrs. Le Cortez."

The social worker glanced over the artist's shoulder, noticing that the crow in the painting was in flight above a Victorian gable, very much like the gable at the top of the Le Cortez home.

"I am an artist," Magdalena said. "As is my daughter. We are by nature both curious and reflective."

Social Worker

Thursday, June 16

Each of the three defendants in the Dobson kidnapping case had been appointed separate lawyers. Renata's lawyer was Mike DeBoer. The social worker knew him as a dependable, competent advocate. But on the morning of June 16, the young lawyer seemed particularly pessimistic about Renata's fate. As the social worker discussed the details of the case with him, he repeatedly shook his head in dismay and rolled his eyes.

"The Dobsons are going after everybody involved, Greta," the lawyer reported glumly. "Police officers, school officials, some poor coach at the high school. Those kids are dead in the water. The boy especially—he's in the most trouble. Everybody assumes he was the leader, and the Xanax and Adderall were from his household. And that weird little one—her *house* was the scene of the crime! Jesus, could these kids have done anything more stupid? This was no ordinary jock they kidnapped! We're talking resident prince of the junior high athletic department, soon to be a high school superstar." He put one palm to his forehead and slowly shook his head.

"So you're saying it looks bad for Renata too?"

"This happened at her *house*, Greta! I'm just saying."

"Keep an open mind, Mike. I'm collecting their journals this afternoon, and I'm anxious to read them because in my opinion there are too many details about the crime that don't make sense."

"Oh, I think it all makes sense. In a twisted kind of way. Three kids on the fringes of junior-high life decide on their own to take down a bully..."

"So you at least agree that Chase Dobson is a bully?"

"It's not illegal to be a bully, Greta. It's very illegal to hold someone against his will and subdue him with drugs."

"That hasn't been proven."

"The suspects aren't denying it."

The social worker's teeth were on edge. "Well...I'm planning to do some digging."

The lawyer shrugged. "Let me know if you find out anything that would help me. As it stands now, I'll work on the no priors and the effects of weeks of bullying on the youngest of the three. It won't be easy."

The social worker backed out of the room as the

lawyer rambled on pitifully. He would be no help at all, she decided. She made her way back to her own office, where two yellow spiral notebooks and a bound sketchbook awaited her. She was drawn to Renata's journal first. Inside the cover she found four drawings in black pen. The first drawing was a map of North Holmes, the second was a scene of Renata in a dark hallway, surrounded by angry boys, the third drawing was a depiction of life in the detention center, and lastly, Renata had drawn her own version of their first meeting.

Each drawing was labeled as a journal entry, and each drawing contained a crow and a fox. "Okay. Okay. Crow and fox," Greta mused. She was unsettled by the drawings—especially the disturbing scene of Renata being bullied at her school—but also impressed. Impulsively, she called security and asked an attendant to bring Renata to her office.

Date: Thursday, June 16

Interview with Renata Le Cortez

From the videotape:

GS: So you're an artist like your mother?

RLC: I'll never be as good as my mother. But I am an artist.

GS: [Sorting through the drawings on her desk] Why did you put a fox in each drawing?

RLC: Magdalena says that everybody has a totem. Whether they know it or not. Hers is a cat.

GS: Ah yes, I noticed a cat. And is yours the fox?

RLC: [Smiles]

GS: As a matter of fact, I met your mother this morning. I stopped at
your house before I came to work.

RLC: You went to my house?

GS: Yes. And I met your mother.

RLC: Was Stefano home?

GS: Your father is apparently out of town.

RLC: Stefano still spends a lot of time in Charlotte. Where we used to
live. He misses . . . people there. Was Magdalena upset?

GS: No. Why would she be upset?

RLC: I don't know. Maybe just because Stefano . . . still needs to go
back to Charlotte.

GS: [After a pause] She seemed happy to be working in her studio.
And she expressed great confidence in you, Renata. She said that
she knows you will do whatever needs to be done to resolve this
situation.

RLC: [A deep sigh] She doesn't believe in worrying. But me, I worry
too much. Which painting was she working on in the studio?

GS: It was a painting of a girl holding onto the back of a crow.

RLC: Ah, the crows.

GS: I noticed that there is also a crow in each of the drawings. Is the
crow another totem?

RLC: Crows symbolize bad luck, Mrs. Shield. I have had some very
bad luck lately.

GS: I see that you have drawn a picture of how terrible that was
for you. Those boys should have been punished. It was very
wrong.

RLC: It was. I still dream about that hallway. I still see their terrible faces and still feel their angry thoughts around me. I feel how much they wanted to hurt me.

GS: And Chase was the worst one, wasn't he?

RLC: May I have my drawings back now, Mrs. Shield? I need to keep them close to me. One drawing continues into another. And I have more inside my head. My mother says artists walk around with drawings and paintings fully formed inside their heads all the time.

GS: Give me a day to make copies of the drawings you've done, and I'll give them back to you tomorrow.

[Renata stands up, ready to leave.]

GS: I wanted to also tell you that I saw the actual room that Chase stayed in at your house, Renata. The laundry room. I looked around it. I sat on the futon. I tried to imagine what it must have been like for you, having the boy who was your tormentor in a room right next to your bedroom for so many days. I don't know how you stood having him so close. Can you help me to understand that?

RLC: It had to be at my house, Mrs. Shield. That was the only place it would work. But then . . . but then . . . [Grimaces].

GS: Your mother said something interesting this morning. She said that everyone is assuming that Chase was locked in that room against his will. But that maybe it wasn't against his will. Maybe he liked being a prisoner. I wasn't sure what she meant by that. What do you think she meant, Renata?

RLC: I think that even if I had to stay in this place for ten years, Mrs. Shield, I would not be half the prisoner that Chase Dobson is. He is a prisoner in his soul. May I go back to my room now? I'm very tired.

[End of videotape.]

Her work with Renata had taken up most of the morning. Determined to press on, the social worker turned her attention to the second journal, Nate's: *When I arrived in the Hall of Lost Souls, I bravely stood with my GreyMounts, one on either side of me, and as three, we faced our accusers. Bravely, impassively, we heard the words that foretold our imprisonment. We stood united, and we did not falter, and we shed not one tear among us . . . .*

She groaned and lowered her forehead to her desk, resting there a long moment. Then she lifted her head, gave it a shake, and began reading anew.

• • •

Nate loped into the office after his lunch period and perched on the edge of the stuffed chair, happy to see her, eager to begin. He was wearing the first unguarded, full-on smile the social worker had seen on him—it transformed him, made his face radiant, almost angelic. He clasped his hands between his knees and rocked slightly with excitement. "Did I write enough?" he asked. "I write really slowly, see, because I try to make every single word perfect."

His journal lay open on her desk, the lettering so tiny, belabored, and regular that it almost appeared to be typed. "No, the length is fine. It's just that . . . "

"I'm a fantasist, Mrs. Shield. I guess I should have told you that last week. I've written stories before about Grey-Mounts. Did you like what I wrote?"

"Nathaniel." Greta chose her words carefully. "This

isn't really a question of me liking or not liking your writing. This was not a creative writing assignment. I needed you to write about what *happened*."

"I am writing about what happened," he insisted. "Swear to God, Mrs. Shield. This is the way I write."

The two stared at each other. The boy's expression grew more concerned; he was unhappy to have disappointed her. "You don't think I'm a good writer?"

"I think that you're a very good writer. Remarkable, actually. I just wish that you had written about things . . . more directly."

Nate shook his head, disagreeing with her. "That's not what you said, Mrs. Shield. You said write about how it all began. That's what I'm trying to do, but it's really complicated."

"Why can't you just tell me what happened?"

He lowered his head, withholding. She sighed and looked over the notes she had typed on her computer screen. "All right then, since this is what we have to work with, let me just get a few details straight. Your father doesn't live with you and you're not very close with your mother or your sister, correct?"

"That's kind of an understatement."

"You consider Katie and Renata to be your sisters?"
Nodded.

"And Chase Dobson had a history of harassing girls at the junior high, and this is something you observed him doing to other girls long before he targeted Renata?"

Nodded.

"Also he puts something into his Gatorade pretty regularly?"

Silence, but no disagreement.

"Do you know what's in the flask?"

Nate thought a moment, as though deciding if it was safe to tell her this. "Vodka," he said finally. "Sometimes mixed with Adderall, sometimes just vodka."

"You're sure about this? About Chase bringing this . . . potion . . . with him to school?"

A silent nod.

"Do other people at school know about this?"

"His friends know it. I knew it. I'm not his friend, but I watched him. You know, during my Year of Watchfulness."

"Right. Right. Okay two more things. You say you very much like Katie's mother, but you called Renata's mother a . . ." She looked for the correct word. ". . . a 'sorceress.' Why did you call her that?"

"Well . . . she's an artist and her art is kind of spooky. It's all over their house. I mean, if you saw it for yourself . . . "

"That's all you meant? That she's a spooky artist?"

Another nod.

"Fine. One more thing. That time you describe when you were alone with Chase . . . he told you something that nobody else knows?"

The boy was becoming uncomfortable. His smile was gone; he looked trapped. "It's better if I just keep writing," he said.

"Can you just tell me . . . did you two have some kind of a relationship? You can tell me that, Nathaniel, you can trust me."

His expression changed, became impatient. "I'm not gay, Mrs. Shield. If I was gay, I would just say it."

"I'm not suggesting that you're gay. But you are implying in your journal that some kind of exchange happened. Last year. Before all this trouble with Renata began. Right?"

He was slouched in the chair now, away from her, clearly unwilling to elaborate further on what he had written.

"Okay. Is there anything else you can tell me about Chase and the flask?"

Eyes closed. "His grandfather gave it to him. His name was Chase too. Chase Dobson the First. His dad is the Second. Chase and his grandfather were really close. That's all I'm going to say."

"Nathaniel . . ."

"But I'll keep writing about what happened, okay? How about I just keep going with my journal?"

The social worker sighed. "All right, then. Keep going. By all means."

He exhaled, relieved. The smile returned. "Did you like how I call you *The Great She?*"

"That was a nice touch. But my job right now is not to praise your writing. My job is to be your advocate. I'm here to help you to come to terms with what you are accused of. And to prepare you for your next appearance in court, which is not so very far away. I am starting to get a little worried about it. I honestly think all three of you should also be more worried."

"Oh, I'm worried," Nate insisted quietly. He leaned forward in his chair, moving his shoulders closer to her, and the social worker had a sense of his length and his strength, something she hadn't really assessed before, because he had been so hunched and passive in their earlier interview. She tensed involuntarily—a reflex from years of dealing with young male delinquents. But the expression on his face reassured her. She had the distinct feeling that he liked her. He spoke earnestly. "We made a pact, Mrs. Shield."

"I figured as much, Nathaniel. But here's the thing." She closed her eyes again, surprised to find herself close to tears. *I must be overtired*, she thought. She quickly regained her composure and moved in a different direction. "Tell me a little bit more about your father, Nathaniel. Does he know the trouble you're in?"

"My dad doesn't have anything to do with what happened."

"I'd like you to tell me about him anyway. Could you please write a little more about your relationship with him? Maybe a memory or two? Can I count on you to do that?"

He agreed with the merest nod. But as he stood up to leave, he asked, "Can I please have your permission to write at night, Mrs. Shield? In my room?"

"That's simply not possible, Nathaniel. Write when you can."

He looked crestfallen. His body sagged momentarily into the chair. He asked plaintively, "Do you know where I could get one of those rollerball-type pens? A black one or a blue one? I think I could write faster if I had one. They're so much better for getting the words to flow."

The social worker happened to have one in her purse. "You'll still need to turn this back in to your Shift Supervisor," she said. "I'll let him know I gave it to you."

The pen cheered him instantly. "Thank you so much," he said. "You have no idea how much this pen will help me."

• • •

The coach from the junior high remembered her. "Greta Shield! From the JDC, right? My wife speaks very highly of you. She says you're the go-to person for messed-up kids in the area."

She ignored the praise. "Right now, I'm working with the kids who abducted Chase Dobson."

His voice hushed with concern. "Oh my God, those *crazy* kids—what were they thinking? Are you calling to ask me about the Le Cortez girl?"

"You know Renata?"

"I do. I also teach a few science courses at the junior high and Renata came into my advanced biology class last fall, halfway through the semester. Odd-looking girl, very bright. I never would have assumed she was dangerous.

She was kind of in her own world, didn't interact much with the other students."

"Did she interact with you?"

"A little bit. I think she liked my class, especially after I complimented her on her artwork. She did some incredibly creative science assignments. But the other kids thought she was strange, definitely."

"Did she sometimes turn in a drawing in place of a more conventional assignment?"

"She did! Which I didn't discourage since she always got A's on her tests and quizzes. She knew her biology. Like I said, very smart. God, it's hard for me to imagine her in prison. How is she taking it?"

"It's not prison, Martin," Greta corrected. "It's detention for juveniles. There's a big difference."

"Right. So how is she handling being locked up over there?"

"It hasn't been an easy time for her, I can tell you that. Her friends seem to be handling it better, perhaps because they come from less privileged backgrounds."

"Well . . . I want you to know that I welcome any opportunity to help Renata. I would be happy to share my impressions about what happened to her. The whole . . . harassment thing . . . it happened in the hallway right outside my lab."

A long pause. The social worker kept her voice neutral. "It would be very helpful to speak with you," she said. "Especially because I was originally calling you about your connection to Chase Dobson. You are his tennis and soccer coach, is that correct?"

"Yes, unfortunately."

"Why unfortunately?"

"Chase had become really difficult, exhibiting more and more temper throughout the spring. I felt that it was adversely affecting team morale."

"Oh, we do need to talk," the social worker said.

He agreed to meet her for lunch on Saturday morning after his morning doubles match. Her excitement about this was interrupted by the intercom. Security announced that Claire Havenga was again in the reception area, requesting yet another meeting with her.

. . .

Claire was dry-eyed and composed. She even managed a weak smile. "Just for a moment, Greta?"

Katie's unexamined journal was on top of the others and the social worker nonchalantly covered it with a folder. "What can I help you with today, Claire?"

Claire shut the door behind her. "Have you had a chance to read Katie's journal?"

"No, I have not."

"No matter. I mostly wanted to apologize for my call this morning. I should never have called you while I was still so upset. You must think I'm an emotional disaster. In my job I handle all sorts of situations and confrontations. I hope you don't think I have no professional skills."

"I don't think that at all. I know how concerned you are about Katie."

"I just wanted to ask you straight out if my daughter is cooperating with you. Are you finding her difficult to deal with?"

"She has not been uncooperative, Claire. Not at all. I believe that we are making progress. I'm planning to read her journal now and meet with her before the end of the day."

"Okay. Okay. Listen, if you do learn anything helpful . . . anything that would help me to understand why . . . "

"The journals are confidential," the social worker said firmly. "This is something that I always promise my residents. Without exception. It's an important part of establishing trust."

"No, I was just thinking that . . . when you do get a chance to read it . . . if there is anything that you think might help me to . . . "

"I need my residents to trust me," Greta insisted. "It's a fragile process, Claire."

"I know it's a fragile process. I have my girls keep journals too. It's just that . . . it's just that . . . she used to trust *me*."

"We have the same goal, Claire. Please believe that."

Claire nodded, barely. Then she stood up and said good-bye, somewhat defeatedly.

The social worker turned immediately to Katie's journal. She read the first page with a sinking feeling. *I guess they call it a pod because we are like the peas that are separated from other peas in the other pods or whatever.*

Greta flipped through the brief pages—all about Katie's first week in detention—all pointless. Her mind flooded with aggravation. She looked at the clock. It was 4:00 P.M.; the students were out of school. Katie would most likely be in the gym, but no matter. Greta picked up the phone, called the control desk staff desk, and asked the Shift Supervisor to bring Katie to her office.

First greyMount Katie

Lee Ann must have told Mrs. Shield that I have been writing A LOT in my journal, Journal, way more than what I turned in, those six lame pages in the fake one. I told her that I threw a bunch of pages away because my first journal entries were very poor-quality writing. She said she doesn't want me to throw anything away from now on. She wants to see every word I write, and she told me that the pages I handed in were extremely disappointing. I wanted to tell her the truth, Journal—that now I have two journals and the important one is hiding under the mattress in my room. But of course I didn't. I just sat there like a statue while she acted all disappointed and worried about me.

Now I feel terrible—Mrs. Shield is totally trying to help me! It brought back memories of disappointing my mom, which started happening after I became best friends with Renata, but that wasn't my fault either! Mom had this grudge against Renata that was so UNREASONABLE! I secretly think it was because she didn't like me having a girlfriend that I wanted to hang out with more than I wanted to hang out with her. She was never that way about Nate. She liked him from the very beginning. With Renata, she would always make snide remarks about how she dressed or how she wasn't any fun and it was really immature, Journal, and then we would start arguing and honestly, we never fought about anything before that. We got along fine. Even though I was already starting to think that she was way too nosy and involved in my friendship with Nate. But we didn't fight about it.

So Mrs. Shield hands me back the fake journal, and then she asked me why I don't trust her, and I didn't know what to say because I do trust her. But there is just no way that I can tell her what really happened. Or show her the real journal. Or say anything about what's in it. Already there are too many things I've written down that no one can ever see.

After she told me she was disappointed in me, there was this long, awkward silence. Just to say something, anything, I asked her if she had read Renata's journal too.

*Mrs. Shield: Renata's journal is no concern of yours. You
need to be more worried about your own journal.*

She sounded really annoyed with me. But at least she
wasn't yelling or grabbing my head like someone else I
could mention. I told her that lately I can't stop worrying
about Renata. More and more every day. I told her it was
hard for me to imagine that Renata was doing okay.

*Me: I was only thinking that maybe if you've seen Renata's
journal, you might be able to tell me how she's doing.*

*Mrs. Shield: I might if she had actually written
something!*

*Me: Did she make drawings instead of writing? Did you
LOVE them?*

*Mrs. Shield: No, I did not love them. There seems to be
some sort of a news blackout with you three.
I don't know what I'm going to do about
it. We have very little time left before your
court date!*

From this I could tell that she wasn't happy with Nate's
journal either. Which means that both of them are keeping the pact!

I hid that I was insane with relief. I felt so proud of
them, especially Renata! But maybe it showed on my face
because right then Mrs. Shield put her nose way closer to
mine than usual, and it was too much like what my mom

does, so I leaned back and pressed myself into the puffy chair to get some space between us.

Mrs. Shield: You kids need my HELP! Do you understand? You need my HELP!

She was almost yelling at me! I got really silent, wishing I could disappear. Then she told me that our time was up, like she was kicking me out for bad behavior. I practically ran out of her office. I wasn't relieved anymore—I felt terrible. I felt like a criminal, and I am NOT a criminal. And then I got this huge need to write in my journal, Journal. I mean the real one. This one. Like if I didn't write some of these feelings down right away, I might lose my mind. I might explode into pieces.

But I had to wait until after dinner. I had to wait until right now. Tomorrow night, I swear, I will write about the party. About the night we took him. It will be movie night, but I don't even care. I'm just going to skip movie night, no matter what the movie is. I have to write this out. I have to remember. Like Mrs. Shield says, I have to be more worried about myself.

Nathaniel, Son of James

Journal
Day Twelve of Captivity

Morning: The Great She has asked me to address my bloodline, to explain why James of Cleves has not come to my aid during my time of imprisonment. She does not understand that I do not need to see my father in order to feel his spirit with me, nor hear his voice to feel his presence, nor behold his face in order to know that he smiles when he thinks of me. He is watching me in my tribulations, guiding me, having none but the utmost faith in me. I know that he is aware of my sorrows and that he suffers with me. Understand, Great She, that he is gone, but not gone. He is far away, but ever near.

I am my father's most beloved offspring; I have always known it. More than anyone he understands the path I have chosen and how it has led me to this place of exile. He believes in me, he knows that I am steadfast and that I will not falter, nor be discouraged by the ignorance and privation of his other children, including the one who calls herself my sister. I do not waste my energy with thoughts of them, they no longer matter to my quest. They are the pawns of she who bore me, but I am beyond the reach of the Queen of Shadows at last.

James of Cleves will never return to North Holmes. He will never be fooled into coming back to the site of his undoing. He will not turn back. He reigns in a place not of this world. Never again will he allow himself to be disgraced by she who once called herself his wife, she who sleeps in a bed of delusions, wrapped in blankets of desperation and chaos.

His ancestors were Danes, Great She, and because of this he has the height, fair hair, and strong profile of his forefathers, men of great wisdom, courage, and fine minds. They came to the northern regions to settle the great forests and stayed to become artists and scientists. James carries within his mind the ability to see buildings in empty space, stairwells and towers and glass and stone borders and metal beams in a blank landscape. He is what is called an architect, Great She. In Cleves, he flourishes.

His ascendance began only after he escaped from North Holmes, passing willingly into a time of exile in the Middle Regions, until at last he settled in the great city of Cleves, a place of prosperity, where he resumed his chosen profession—designing buildings that shimmer and move as they reflect sunlight, towering over the great Erie Sea. His buildings came to life in his new city, solidifying name and reputation; whereas in North Holmes, he malingered and hid, trapped in his miserable union, beleaguered by undeserving, unwanted children. Except for me, of course.

He was wise to leave, Great She. In Cleves he dwells in a tower of his own design. I have not seen him in many years, but I have proof of these things. Photographs he has sent to me. Letters describing many challenges and triumphs he has sent to me.

You ask me for a memory: here is one.

When I was six, James of Cleves decided that it was time I learned to swim in the deep waters of my homeland. During the summer of that year, James and I rode our bikes to the southern shores of the Michigan sea until we came to a small stretch of private shoreline, belonging to a friend of his youth. There James instructed me in the different methods of swimming—crawl, butterfly, and backstroke. I remember clearly how he demonstrated in the shallows the techniques for each of these methods. I remember that it was late in the summer and that the water was warm and clean and different in color every day. My father would take me by the hand and lead me from the shallows until we were deep enough that I could barely touch bottom. I was not then afraid of deepwater as I am today, for his bravery was my bravery. We were alone,

Great She. He did not take my sister, and my brothers were not yet born. My father had decided that I was ready to follow in his footsteps and become a great swimmer, a champion, winner of medals and trophies for speed and stamina. But I don't think that was his only reason for taking me to the sea.

I think my father was realizing that life in North Holmes was unbearable for him. Perhaps he sensed the time of exile was coming and he wanted to teach me something that had been important to his own survival. After he had instructed me in his most gentle and expert manner as to the proper way of using my arms and legs in the deepwater, he would ask me to sit in the sand and watch him as he swam from one buoy to the next on that small stretch of beach. He swam back and forth for a very long time, and I would sit at the water's edge and feel his energy flowing into me from across the water. And now I believe that this was his way of saying good-bye to me. And wishing me safe journey in the years to come, which he must have already known I would have to endure without him.

I can still feel the strength of his mighty arm as he led me out to the deepwater for my swimming lesson. And I can see the movement of his hands and shoulders as he swam parallel to the shore. This memory is a great comfort to me now, Great She. I summon it whenever I feel lost or like I don't have the strength I need to endure my long imprisonment.

Still Morning: I have noticed that my fellow prisoners all speak of their fathers—if they indeed know their fathers—with anger, casting blame upon them, weaving tales of cruelty, abandonment, and terrible deprivations. This happens during the times when we must all sit in a circle and address the darkness that has led us all to this place—the reasons we are not free—which is impossible for me, because I have not failed in my quest to be a noble warrior, but rather succeeded. I am the exiled son of an exile, and I have prevailed, and so I remain silent during these times, revealing nothing.

I will tell you in confidence, Great She, what the Master once revealed to me about his own father—a man known far and wide in North Holmes, a legend. This the Master told me himself, but without pride or affection. He told me that his father had once reigned supreme in the arenas and fields of North Holmes, and that decades before, his father's father had also reigned. He was the Patriarch, the first Chase Dobson, the first athlete in a line of champions, ever triumphant in the early days of the village. There is a room in the House of Dobson that is filled with the trophies of three generations, starting with the Patriarch. I have not actually seen this room with my own eyes, only heard it described by the Master. The

Patriarch, now departed, long ago triumphed over all who challenged him. He never faltered or doubted his nobility, as the Master did during the time of our first meeting in the little room. The Patriarch was unflinching, unfailing, ever victorious for his entire life. This is what the Master told me. And during that time he acquired great wealth and many mansions and three wives, Great She. His reign was supreme, this much I know. More I cannot say.

My father was a champion in a different way, a solitary way—a way of clean, silent movement—a swimmer! He moved through water like a knife, easily and without confusion; this was a balm for the torment of his final days of captivity, before he escaped into the Middle Regions and found freedom there, and fortune, and left me alone, and bereft, but I understand, Great She, I understand.

Social Worker

Saturday, June 19

The coach was tan, fit, and more broad-shouldered than the social worker remembered. She stayed seated at her café table, hoping he would recognize her from afar, which he did. He strode to her table and set his briefcase on an empty chair. He shook her hand warmly. "So good to see you again, Greta. Sorry I'm late."

He pulled a drawing from his briefcase—scribbly and intricate, a series of fantastical creatures, drawn in a style she immediately recognized.

"It's a cell diagram," Martin said. "Final project from last semester. As you can see, Renata put her own spin on it."

The social worker studied the drawing. Each element of the animal cell—the mitochondria, the cilia, the tubules—had morphed out of the cell membrane into actual fantastic creatures including speech balloons about what role they play in cell biology. It made the social worker smile.

"Pretty cool, right? I gave her an A and asked her if I could keep it."

"She is very creative."

"Like I said on the phone, I just can't picture this girl in prison."

The social worker resisted the impulse to correct the coach. She pictured her last glimpse of Renata, the way she had scurried from her office in her oversized sweats, the hair at the back of her head, matted and forlorn. Like a prisoner.

They ordered and made small talk until Greta asked, "Can you tell me more about what happened to Renata outside your classroom? With Chase and those other boys?"

The coach's tone was rueful. "Sometimes I could hear the commotion in the hall. And I knew some of the other boys who were involved. Mostly football players. A couple of boys from the tennis team."

"And you didn't stop them?"

He drew back slightly at her tone. "This sort of thing goes on all the time, Greta. Sure, I would go out into the hallway and bark at the boys from time to time, tell them to grow up, quit being jerks, but you can't really stop them. You know the way boys are at that age."

Greta lowered her head, pretending to be suddenly engrossed in her bagel. Finally she said, "Let's talk about Chase."

"Right. Chase. *Charles* Dobson the *Third*. One of the finest tennis players I have ever coached. An excellent soccer player. A born competitor. But as I mentioned, he was starting to have a disruptive effect on the other players. I noticed back in March that some of the other boys were afraid of him. I didn't like seeing that—it really affects morale. And then . . . before I could take action . . . he disappeared."

He glanced at his watch.

"Do you have another appointment?" Greta asked. She still had many questions to ask him.

"I do. But we can talk again. What I mostly wanted to say to you this morning is that I would really like to help you with this . . . situation with Renata. As a way of helping her. Maybe I should have done more for her."

"Maybe," Greta agreed calmly. "I could definitely use a contact at the school, somebody who's willing to see beyond the police reports."

"Where would you like to start?"

"I'm trying to figure out exactly what happened on the night Chase disappeared. He was taken from a local party, according to police reports."

"I'll tell you this much," the coach insisted. "When I first read about it in the paper, I thought that some of the details didn't add up. For instance—how did the boy—that Wilson boy—how would he have convinced Chase to leave Luke Misner's party if they didn't already know each other?"

"So you know the boy who threw the party?"

"Luke Misner, I do. He was on the 8th grade tennis team, briefly. Terrible player. He got discouraged and quit early. Nice kid, though. Really surprised to hear he'd throw a party like that. No supervision, alcohol flowing. That's what I heard anyway."

"Can you contact him and ask him more about his party?"

"Wouldn't the police have already done that?"

"Probably, but you might be able to find out more than the police. Coaches are so important to boys. He may still want your approval. Ask him if he remembers seeing Nate Wilson at his party. And speaking of Nate, do you know anything about him?"

He shook his head. "When the story first broke, I looked him up in the yearbook—the girl too—Katie somebody—but I didn't recognize either of them. They aren't on any school teams."

"But you do know Renata and you know Chase. And you'll talk to Luke Misner. That is going to be such a help to me."

"I'll call you just as soon as I have something to tell you."

He stood up to leave.

"One more thing," she requested. "I would very much like to actually *see* Chase Dobson. I've met his mother, but she won't allow me to see him, even with a lawyer present. I'm really good at reading teenagers, Martin. Chase's role in this whole thing is starting to feel like a missing piece of the puzzle."

"Let me get back to you on that. I'll see what I can do."

She gave him her card and thanked him again. He picked up Renata's cell diagram and hurried away.

Although it was Saturday, she drove to her office, where she pulled the copies of Renata's drawings from her file, gazing in particular at the drawing of their first meeting, Renata, sad and shrunken in the stuffed chair. A fox watched from the window. The entire right side of the page was filled with her profile.

Unsettled, Greta focused on something she hadn't paid attention to before—the earring on the line of her ear—a dangling hoop made of bone. Despite her tears and protestations, Renata had noticed the social worker's earrings, one of the few presents that her ex-husband had ever bought for her. Bone earrings from a museum shop from the one who left her.

First GreyMount Katie

I am trying to remember Nate's exact words, Journal. He was trying to convince us that we should go to the party to get Chase, that awful party, the kind of party nobody ever invites kids like us to, not even before we got stung.

Swear to God, right then and there I told both of them that it was a really bad idea, I didn't want to go anywhere near Luke Misner's cottage. My mom warned me about those kinds of parties—no parents anywhere and everybody gets really hammered and then half the people there puke off the side of the deck and there are like two hundred rumors about who hooked up for weeks afterward. I told them there was no way I was going up there.

Nate: You guys don't have to actually go inside, just wait up here for us. I'll find Chase myself and bring him out and then we can take him over to Renata's.

I asked him why he was so sure that Chase would talk to him—or that he could even get past Chase's bodyguards. (I guess they're not really "bodyguards," but they're football guys who are always around Chase. Whatever. I don't understand boys.)

Nate: If we wait until after midnight, everyone will be so drunk that they won't try to stop me.

God, it was such a terrible idea.

Meanwhile I was noticing that Renata and Nate kept looking at each other—the kind of look where you can tell they discussed some of this stuff before. They discussed this plan without me, Journal! My two best friends in the whole world!

Nate: No one will see me. I'll become invisible. I'll sneak into the cottage and they won't even know I'm there.

We were all standing under the streetlights in the parking lot for the public beach. Nate and Renata looked slightly yellow from the lights. From maybe 500 yards away, at the edge of the public beach, we could hear the party. I lost it then. I started yelling at both of them. Why did Nate want to do this crazy thing? Why was Renata going along with it? How could they have planned it without me?

Renata was being really quiet. I wondered if she was getting scared too. But then when she spoke, it was with her *I'm-in-charge* voice.

> *Renata: Nate is right. We need to do this. We need to be there for each other like never before. Nate will go inside, and you and I will wait outside. It's settled, Katie.*

I started to say something, but Renata stepped forward and took my pleading hands with her little hands. She has really strong hands, Journal; you wouldn't believe how strong.

> *Renata: We're going to do something huge tonight, Katie. We're going to prove something once and for all to all the Chase Dobsons of the world. Will you help us? Will you?*

Renata squeezed my big hands inside her small ones and it was like an electric current went through me. A blast of her courage passed into me. I looked into her brown, brown eyes and then I looked into Nate's blue, blue eyes. My two best friends and they both seemed so sure. And suddenly I knew I had to be part of it. I hoped they were right, but I decided that I had to be part of it anyway. Because I really am the strongest one. I mean physically, not mentally. I'm really tall and my whole life, boys have been afraid of me. My mom isn't tall and strong like me so I guess I must have got that from my dad, whoever he was.

I guess he was big. I guess he was a bully, like Chase Dobson, but I don't want to think too much about that. I'm not a bully but I'm stronger than Nate. Sometimes he calls me his GreyMount, which is a word he made up that means warrior. That's how he sees me, Journal. So how could I say no to him? How could I not help my friends? I don't even exist without them.

• • •

Nate walked away from the parking lot. We watched him head toward the cottage, to the bottom of two flights of wooden stairs. Then he started going up the stairs—so many stairs, up and up and up—and I was so scared for him. He climbed with his head down and his hood up, maybe so that no one would recognize him or try to stop him, and then he was on the second story and he walked along this one long stretch of deck where a few really big guys were standing around outside and nobody stopped him and then he disappeared—gone—inside the party house.

I tried to be patient. I watched the time on my cell phone, checking every minute. It took ten. Then all of a sudden there was Nate walking back down the steps. With somebody walking behind him. And then they came toward us, away from the cottage. It was Chase, Journal. Nate was walking with Chase. At first, I couldn't believe my eyes. I looked at Renata then, and I saw that she was shivering, but not from cold.

Something was wrong with Chase, Journal. He was

actually kind of leaning against Nate, having some trouble standing up by himself. His mouth was hanging open in a strange, zombie way.

Me: He looks pretty messed up, Nate.

Nate: I know.

Chase made a strange sound, like a moan.

Me: What's wrong with him, Nate?

Nate: He's drunk. And he was a little freaked out to see me.

Chase: Where are we going?

Nate: We're going to walk a little way to Renata's house and then you can relax, okay? Don't worry, Katie. He's not dangerous.

Chase: Come on—you said you'd help me!

Chase's hair was all stringy and messy. His pupils were dilated. His skin looked even worse under the lights than ours did. He was sweating. He finally noticed Renata and me, and he squinted at us over Nate's shoulder.

Chase: Shit, Man, you didn't tell me you were bringing your girlfriends.

Renata: We're not his girlfriends. We're his friends. Not that you would know anything about having friends.

Suddenly Chase started to breathe really fast. Like almost gasping. Like something was kicking in, some drug or other. Or was he starting to cry?

Chase: [Breathing all heavy] But you're my friend, right, Nate? Right?

Nate: Come on. Walk with me. Only a few blocks.

He put one arm around Chase's shoulder. Then we all started to walk. Every few minutes, Chase's cell phone rang—a weird ring tone that sounded like a dog barking. It made us all very jumpy. Finally, when we were walking past a Dumpster, Chase swore at his own ring tone, squinted at the text, and then threw the phone into the trash. None of us said another word as we walked down Lakeshore and up the hill, all the way to Renata's house.

Personal time is over. I have to go to the gym.

Social Worker

Sunday, June 20

The social worker was back in the office on Sunday, checking reports of her residents' behavior, noting who had recently had visitors, and who had upcoming court appearances. She often worked on Sundays to keep from falling behind.

At noon, as she was exiting the building, she spied an oddly familiar-looking girl, walking her bicycle toward the building from the near-empty north parking lot. The girl lowered her eyes, avoiding the social worker's gaze, keeping her head down until they had passed each other. Greta was intrigued enough to follow. With a few yards between them, they headed toward the detention center's main entrance. The girl glanced back, saw the social worker a short distance behind her, and quickened her pace.

In that glance, Greta realized what was familiar about this girl—she bore such a striking resemblance to Nate Wilson that if she had been dressed like a boy, the social worker might have assumed it *was* Nate. But Nate's sister was wearing a cotton top with puffy sleeves and a short denim skirt, her long, bare legs ending in white sandals. She looked aggressively feminine.

"Excuse me!" the social worker called.

"I'm a visitor!" the girl called back, still moving her bicycle toward the JDC. "My brother's inside!" Her voice was also jarringly familiar—the same voice she'd heard on the telephone at the Wilson household, a chattier, higher-pitched version of Nate's. But now, in the parking lot, she sounded anxious, afraid of being stopped. The social worker noticed that the basket on the front of her bike held a paperback New Revised Standard Version of the Bible.

While she locked her bike around a lamppost in the parking lot, Greta closed the distance between them. "You must be Natalie!" she said. "I am so happy to finally meet you. I'm Nathaniel's social worker—I spoke to you on the phone. I'm Greta Shield."

The girl studied Greta. "You're the one who called?" she asked.

"I am. And I know that you're Nathaniel's sister."

A pause. "He probably didn't say anything nice about me, right?"

"Well . . . he hasn't said much about anyone in his family. But he'll be pleased to have a visitor. The entrance is that way."

Natalie started walking again, now clutching the thick paperback.

Back in her car, the social worker started her engine just long enough to cool the interior and waited. Twenty minutes later, Natalie came out, walking back into the parking lot with the same breezy determination. The social worker stood up beside her car and waved. "Did you find him all right, Natalie?" she called.

"I did. It went okay." She came closer. "Is a social worker the person who helps kids get out of here faster?"

"I'm doing my best, Natalie. Maybe you can help too."

"I doubt it. Plus I have to be going. I'm babysitting my little brothers in an hour."

"I understand. I'm glad you came. I've been hoping to meet someone from Nathaniel's family."

The girl grimaced. "Why do you keep calling him Nathaniel?"

"Because . . . that's what he asked me to call him."

"He asked you to call him *Nathaniel*? That is seriously weird, Ma'am. Nobody calls him Nathaniel. He's just . . . he's Nate."

"Neither of your parents call him Nathaniel?"

She shook her head. "If he told you they did, it's another lie."

An uncomfortable pause. The social worker tried

again, "I was wondering about your mother."

"She won't come. She can't handle this place. And Nate doesn't want to see her anyway."

"He told you that?"

"I just know. They don't get along. I didn't want to come either, to tell you the truth. I mean, I feel sorry for him, being stuck in juvie, even though he acts like it's no big deal. He doesn't care what it's like for Mom and me. It's pretty embarrassing at my school and my church when people ask me how long he's in for. Or why he did it."

"Do you mean . . . why he kidnapped Chase Dobson?"

"Well . . . *yeah*, that's what he did, isn't it?"

"His guilt hasn't been proven, Natalie. What do you think?"

She twisted a strand of white blonde hair—a gesture Greta had seen Nate do many times. "Well . . . he acts like he did it. Or at least he acts like he doesn't care if people think he did it. So I guess he probably did it. And those two girls . . . those girls he was hanging out with, they're not nice girls, Ma'am. They might have talked him into it." She shrugged and leaned over to unlock her bike. "Really, I have to get back."

"Do you think we could talk some more about this, Natalie?"

"Maybe . . . I don't know." She took a few steps away, then turned and blurted, "There's something wrong with my brother. He lives in a dream world, writing those weird stories."

Greta dug in her purse for a business card. Natalie pocketed it dutifully. "What do *you* think is wrong with your brother, Natalie?"

Natalie shrugged. "We used to be really close, you know. We used to do things together. Then he changed. I pray for him. Me and Mom, we pray every night for him to change back."

"Change back to what?"

"To how he was before he went to Cleveland."

A slight pause. "Nate went to Cleveland?"

A nod.

"Recently?"

"Last year. He didn't tell anybody he was going. He just one day took the bus by himself instead of going to school. We didn't know where he was. I don't even know where he stayed. He said he didn't stay with my dad. He was there for like three days and ever since he came back he's been like a different person. Wouldn't talk to me about what happened, wouldn't go to church with us, wouldn't pray. I don't know what it was, Mrs. Shield, but I think something bad might have happened to him while he was in Cleveland."

"Didn't your mother try to find out what might have happened? Did she speak about it with your father?"

At this mention of her mother and father, Natalie seemed to realize that she had already said too much. She frowned, upset with herself. "Wow, I really didn't mean to talk this long, Ma'am. Now I'm really late. I have to go, sorry." She climbed onto her bike and pedaled away.

The social worker called after her, "Call me anytime you want to talk, okay? You have my number . . . ."

. . .

Back inside, Greta found Nate in his room with his door ajar. He was propped on one elbow, the length of him end-to-end on his narrow cot, writing in his journal with the roller pen she had given him. When he saw her, he closed his notebook, sat up straight, and slid his feet back into the scuffs at his bedside.

"At ease," she insisted. "We're not going anywhere. I just wanted to mention that I noticed you had a visitor."

He scowled.

"She rode her bike all the way out here by herself, Nathaniel. That couldn't have been easy for her. She must have really wanted to see you."

He gestured to the foot of his bed, where the paperback Bible now lay atop a folded blanket. "She brought me some inspirational reading material."

"I see that. But weren't you the least bit happy to see her? She's the only person from your family who's come out here."

"She was hoping I'd fall on my knees and pray with her, Mrs. Shield. That's why she came."

A pause. Greta tried going in a different direction. "Did your father have a problem with how religious your mother and your sister are?" she asked.

Nate picked up the closed notebook and put it into his lap, as though protecting it. "I was just writing some things about my dad," he said. "I think you're going to really like my new pages."

"I hope so. And are you writing about your trip to Cleveland?"

His jaw dropped. "How did you know I went to Cleveland?"

"Your sister mentioned it."

Now he looked appalled. "You *talked* to her?"

"I ran into her in the parking lot."

Nate was now holding the journal stiffly, close to his chest, unmistakably upset. "If you talk to my sister, Mrs. Shield, then you will only hear lies about me."

"Did you visit your father in Cleveland last year?"

He pursed his lips together, lifted his chin, and met her eyes. "I went to Cleveland, but I didn't see my father."

Greta hid her concern that he was lying to her and changed the subject. "Why did you ask me to call you Nathaniel if everyone else calls you Nate?"

The question deepened his distress. He looked away.

"Nate, why did you ask me to call you something no one else calls you?"

A silence. Finally he said, his face still turned from her. "Because Nathaniel can handle being in here. This place. Nathaniel can survive in here."

"But Nate can't?"

No answer.

"Nate?"

"It just . . . helps me when you call me Nathaniel." He gestured toward his notebook. "It inspires me." His voice was clogged; she thought he might be close to tears.

"Go back to your journal, then," she instructed. "But I want you to explain in your journal why you think your sister would lie to me. Will you do that, Nathaniel?"

He nodded sadly, then lay back on his cot and looked at the ceiling. The closed notebook slid from the cot to the cement floor. He was waiting for her to leave.

• • •

Back in her car, her cell phone rang, and it was the coach from the junior high. "I know it's Sunday, but are you busy?"

"Not really," she said. "Why?"

"I'm at the junior high. Can you meet me here?"

"I'll be there in ten minutes."

• • •

North Holmes Junior High was a new state-of-the-art magnet school in one of the wealthier districts on the west side of the state—a sprawling campus in a 100-acre wooded area just south of North Holmes proper, not terribly far from the JDC. Martin was waiting for her, standing on the curb outside the entrance rotunda. Beyond him were a half dozen doors leading into a mostly glassed-in space that seemed all the more grand and sunlit for being empty. Together, they walked down a high-ceilinged main hallway, their footsteps echoing, to the north wing.

"Not exactly like the school I went to back in Texas," he said proudly.

"Nor mine," the social worker agreed. It was a junior high with the feel of a college campus, including an even more impressive athletic facility than existed at the high school on the other side of town. Many of the teenagers Greta dealt with at the JDC hated the new junior high and had given up trying to feel a part of it, convinced that they weren't welcome.

The coach led her into a small room off the main gymnasium. It was set up with chairs in a half-circle, facing a wall-sized screen. He turned on a computerized projector system. "This is where the various teams study video clips from previous games or matches. I use it a lot with both the tennis team and the soccer team. I thought you might be interested in this."

He lowered the lights and pressed a few keys until the screen expanded. Another click and the players began to move—dozens of teenage boys in soccer uniforms. "From early spring," Martin told her.

As she watched, more soccer players filled the screen with energy and movement. No audio. The boys migrated silently onto the open field.

The coach paused the screen. "Watch this," he instructed, and then pressed play again. "Right there. Watch Chase coming from the right of the screen."

As she watched, a young but broad-shouldered player

ran unhurriedly toward his teammates, angling in from the side of the field farthest from the others. Despite his slow gait, there was a sense of speed and power in his legs, and in the way he kept his shoulders still as he ran. He was prancing, picking up speed slowly. His dark hair was in that kind of half ponytail common to soccer players. The boy was already intensely masculine. A phrase from Nate's journal came to her: *fierce and long-limbed, the master could run for hours . . .*

"Here's something else . . . watch the camera pan the bleachers." The coach paused the video on a shot of the fans, clapping and cheering, although eerily silent. "See that group at the second to the top row of the bleachers? That's the Dobson clan—mother, father, grandmother, and little sister—a budding soccer star in her own right. See how they sit at the center of the tiers, holding court up there? Three generations of superior athletes with young Chase the heir apparent. Notice the patriarch is missing. Chase Senior died in a boating accident last summer—very tragic; you might remember it. It was front-page news."

"I do remember. Wasn't his body found in the channel?"

"Terrible. Up until then, Chase Senior never missed a game. He always sat just slightly above the rest of the family at the very top of the bleachers."

The camera had returned to the group of boys who now encircled their team captain. Greta could clearly see the authority Chase radiated. She watched him consorting with teammates; gesturing them closer for instruction. Still, the footage was too distant for her to get a really clear impression of his face. "Watch him run," the coach instructed quietly. "Like a tiger."

It was true. "Does this look like a boy who could be held for six days against his will?" she wondered aloud.

"The paper mentioned prescription drugs," the coach reminded her. "At least one of those kids knows a thing or two about stealing meds. Have you seen enough of Chase?"

"I think so. Even at a distance, I can see he's a remarkable athlete."

"I'd offer to take you to one of his regular games, but apparently Chase isn't playing on any teams right now. He must be lying low, recovering."

They left the classroom and began walking through the hallway, passing a trio of open double doors to the enormous gymnasium. On impulse, the social worker asked the coach if there was anything resembling a private windowless room off the main locker rooms. The coach thought for a moment and then replied, "There's a cubicle-type area that we use for treating injuries."

"Could I see it?"

"Of course." He led her to the boys' locker room, calling inside first to make sure it was empty. Then he gestured the social worker inside. Hundreds of shiny blue lockers surrounded them. They zigzagged through wooden benches to an area beyond the lockers, where

Greta found a small cubicle, with only a few medicine cabinets on one wall above a hospital-style rolling cot. The social worker stood for a moment in the entryway to this room, trying to picture Nate and the boy she had just seen on the videotape alone in it, sitting on the floor together, exchanging secrets.

"Did something happen in here?" the coach asked.

"I think so," she replied. "Not sure exactly what, though."

They exited the locker room area, passed through the gym, and made their way back to the main hallway, heading to the school's entrance.

On the short walk from the entrance to the parking lot, Greta confessed, "I don't think my kids kidnapped Chase. But what I don't understand is why at least one of them isn't afraid enough of a year in detention to tell me what really happened."

"I hear you. Sounds like they're in big trouble, those kids."

"Speaking of trouble, did you ever get in touch with that boy who had the party?"

"That was the second thing I wanted to tell you. I called Luke Misner and we're meeting tomorrow afternoon to hit a few balls here at the school. I'll give you a call after that."

She agreed to this plan and drove into town to have a late lunch in a café, her thoughts weighed down with the image of Chase Dobson, *The Master*, on the fields of battle at the Great Hall of North Holmes.

Social Worker

Monday, June 21

Martin Collier called first thing Monday morning. "That Luke Misner is a good kid," he said. "He was a hard worker with a good attitude and I liked him. When he left the team, I think he felt like a failure. Maybe enough of a failure to do something as stupid as host an out-of-control party at his parents' summer cottage. Because that wasn't the Luke I knew."

"Was it hard to get him to talk about the night of the party?"

"No, not at all—you were right—he was willing to confide in me. And he told me a few things I think you might find quite interesting."

"Does he remember seeing Nate?"

"He does. Luke doesn't actually know Nate well, but he remembers seeing him that night. Said he came in by himself—the two girls weren't with him. Apparently it was mostly guys at this party, including a lot of high school guys, people Luke didn't know at all, and some were smashed, and Luke was scared. He could see already there'd be hell to pay in the morning. It sobered him up. He remembers what happened very clearly. Nate came at around midnight. Nobody paid much attention to him because there were already so many strangers milling around. But Luke remembers Nate because—as he put it—everybody else was drunk or acting like they were drunk, but this kid was definitely not drunk. Plus, he says that Nate didn't look like the other guys at the party—he said he looked more like a stoner, someone who had accidentally stumbled into the wrong party. Luke was sitting on the couch beside Chase, and he said that Chase had an older girl from Grand Rapids with him; she had more or less passed out in his lap.

"So Luke said that Nate came right up to Chase and just stood in front of him, looking down at him for a long time. No words. Really serious. Luke said Chase had been drinking out of a flask. Nate held out his hand until Chase put the flask in his hand. Then Chase pushed the girl out of his lap and got to his feet and the two of them left the party. According to Luke, Chase totally cooperated."

"Did Luke tell any of this to the police?"

"No. Luke knew that he was already in trouble about the party and he is seriously afraid of Chase. So all he told the police was that Chase was at the party. And that nobody knew exactly when Chase left. The police did a little more questioning and apparently nobody remembered when Chase left. Either they were all too drunk to remember, or else they're all too afraid of Chase to talk about it."

"But Luke definitely saw the two boys leave together?"

"Yes, and get this . . . he says when they passed him, Chase grabbed the front of Luke's shirt and said, 'I wasn't here.' Which is not what Luke told the police. So he's been living in fear of what Chase will do to him ever since."

"He told you that?"

"In so many words. And I've been thinking about what you said at the school yesterday. That those kids couldn't have made Chase do something he didn't want to do. I think you're right."

"What about this flask thing? Did you ever see Chase drinking from a flask?"

"No, but don't forget—I'm his coach. He knows that would have been the end of his athletic career, at least with me. I wouldn't be surprised if he was drinking, though. I've heard that his dad was a big drinker too, back in the day, probably still is. He was, nevertheless, an amazing athlete, went all-state in football and wrestling."

"Hmmm," Greta mused, still thinking about the flask.

"What about this Nate Wilson kid? Does he have a drug problem? Luke called him a stoner."

"There are no drug-related offenses in his history. No *anything* in his history."

"So drugs wouldn't be the connection. What else could it have been? Could they have had some sort of secret relationship? Like a gay thing?"

"I don't think it's that. I think it's something else. Some other kind of secret. Luke's fear of Chase, Martin—did he explain in any way what his fear was based on?"

"Lots of kids are afraid of Chase. Apparently Luke felt very threatened. He was worried that I might turn around and tell Chase about our conversation. I assured him I would not. But he still seemed anxious about it. I got the distinct impression that Chase might have threatened Luke in some way. Some sort of—I don't know—teenage blackmail?"

"What makes you say that?"

"The way Luke was acting. Like he was definitely telling me things he hadn't told anyone else, but I also sensed that there were also a lot of things he *wasn't* telling me. Being very careful not to tell me."

"Martin, would you mind talking to him again? Maybe he'll tell you more."

"Right away?"

"The sooner the better. I have to step things up with this case. The whole thing will be out of my hands very soon. After which it will all come down to a couple of lawyers who may not be willing to stand up to the Dobsons."

"Okay, I'll call him tomorrow. Anything else?"

"One more favor. I was wondering if you would consider paying a visit to Renata at the detention center. As a concerned teacher. No one has come to visit her, which bothers me in and of itself, but I was also thinking that she might tell you things that she hasn't told anyone else. Out of gratitude for your concern."

"Am I even allowed to visit her?"

"I will need to get permission from her parents, but I don't think that will be a problem. Visiting times are evenings at 7:00. The only hitch would be if she refuses to see you, but I don't think she would."

"If you think it might help, I'll come tonight."

"Wonderful. See if you can encourage her to talk about the night they took Chase from the party."

. . .

Magdalena's tone was defensive. She asked, "Why would a teacher want to visit my daughter in detention?"

"Because he liked her. And admired her creativity. I also think he feels badly that he did not do more to help Renata when she was being bullied at school." A pause. Greta finished meaningfully, "And because I told him no one has come to visit her yet."

"I see."

"So . . . may I please have your permission to allow Mr. Collier to visit your daughter?"

"Yes. Of course. I hope to visit Renata myself . . . soon." Her voice wavered. She added, "It will not be easy for me."

Greta bit back a retort about detention not being easy for Renata; instead she said calmly, "Well, just give me a call if there's any way that I can help you."

First greyMount Katie

Journal Entry Tuesday, June 22—Lunchtime

As soon as we got him into the laundry room, Journal, he collapsed on a futon that Renata had set up against the wall. Completely crashed out. Nate didn't seem surprised or worried. He kept saying that Chase was fine, everything was fine, almost like he'd seen it all before. But oh my God, me and Renata, we were in total shock. We couldn't believe that it was Chase Dobson passed out cold right in front of us. We stared down at him, in all his horrible hugeness. I know that lots of girls think Chase Dobson is one of the cutest guys in the school, but he didn't look so cute that night; he looked like somebody washed up from a dirty river—his hair was all greasy and he reeked of cigarettes and alcohol. He stank, Journal, if you want the truth. And his snoring was like an old man snoring, full of grunts and snorts and whimpers—disgusting. I couldn't have touched him if my life depended on it. Renata felt the same way. We let Nate take care of him.

Nate unzipped Chase's hoodie and rolled him first on one side to pull the sweatshirt off of him, then to the other side, like he was a doctor in an ER. Did I mention that Chase is gigantic? Underneath the sweatshirt he was wearing a white T-shirt—and he was all soaking wet under his huge arms and another big triangle of sweat on his chest. When Nate was rolling him around, he started groaning, like Nate was hurting him, but he didn't wake up. Then he started to snore even louder.

Me: What is wrong with him?

Nate pulled a silver bottle out of his own back pocket and told me it was Chase's. It had initials etched into the front—CWD.

Nate: He drinks from this, Katie. All the time. His grandfather gave him this flask. Sometimes he puts Adderall in it too.

Me: What's Adderall? And how do you know that? God, how do you know what pills Chase Dobson has in his flask?

Nate and Renata both looked at each other, like they had already talked about this.

Me: Okay, so what do we do with him, you guys? Do we still make him apologize when he wakes up?

Nate: That was the whole point of doing this, Katie.

Renata: He has to apologize.

Me: Why did he say that stuff on the way here about you being his friend, Nate? What was that all about?

Nate: I guess he was just . . . really glad to see somebody he doesn't hate.

Me: Why doesn't he hate you? You seem like exactly the kind of person he would hate. And why don't you hate him back?

Nate: Don't you get it? He came with me of his own free will. Everything depends on what he does from now on.

Me: Are you kidding me? After what he did to Renata? Nate, how could somebody like Chase ever be your friend?

Nate: People change.

Me: Nobody changes that much.

Nate: Katie, people change more than you could ever imagine. Ever. Like in a million years.

We were still standing over Chase. He made such a loud crackling snort that we all jumped.

Me: *What if your mom hears him snoring and comes down here?*

Renata: *This house is soundproof, Katie. Nobody will hear a thing. Trust me.*

Me: *But can you stand it if he sleeps here?*

Renata: *I don't think we have a choice.*

Nate: *I'll stay in here with him. I'll sleep on the floor.*

Me: *If you're staying, I'm staying.*

I started digging in my bag for my cell to call my mom. I asked Nate if he wanted to call his mom.

Nate: *She's been asleep for hours. I don't exactly have a mom who waits up for me.*

Me: *My mom isn't waiting up for me. She just stays up really late.*

Renata: *Stop arguing, you two.*

Me: *What if he wakes up and starts attacking Nate?*

Nate: *Number one, he won't wake up. Number two, he won't attack me. Will you just calm down, Katie?*

Renata: *Come on, Katie, you can sleep in my room. Let Nate deal with Chase.*

She brought Nate a pillow and two blankets. Nate

put one of the blankets over Chase carefully so that he wouldn't wake up. That is the last thing I remember noticing that night—Nate being so gentle, arranging the blanket over Chase's chest. I went into Renata's bedroom then, and we fell asleep in her bed right away. Like instantly. I think we were completely exhausted from our confusion. What were we doing? Honestly thinking back, I'm surprised that we could sleep at all, given how bizarre it was, having Chase Dobson right there with us and Nate sleeping on the floor beside him in case he woke up. None of us knew what was going to happen in the morning. But we were so tired, Journal. Dead tired. We slept like we were as wasted as Chase was.

The next morning the three of us woke up at the same time—around ten. Renata has her own kitchen in her apartment, and so she made us coffee and eggs. Chase snored on, loud enough for us all to hear him in the kitchen, until almost noon, but none of us talked about him. It was like we were pretending he wasn't really there.

Finally we heard him groaning. Then we heard the cot creaking. Then he started coughing.

We got up from Renata's breakfast table and went into the laundry room together. There he was, sitting up on the bed, coughing into his hands. His eyes focused on Nate. He spoke in a raspy voice but it wasn't mean or angry, more confused; he almost sounded like a little boy.

Chase: Where am I?

Nate: You slept here, it's morning.

Chase: I slept here? All night long? Who knows I'm here?

Nate: Nobody. Just us.

Chase: Wow. You really did rescue me. How did I even get here?

Me: Don't you remember? We walked.

Chase: [Looking at me] Who are you? Oh wait. You're one of his girls. The tall one. The one nobody messes with.

Renata was being very quiet, watching Chase, waiting for him to notice her.

Chase: [Squinting at Renata] Uh-oh. You're the little one. That one I . . . shit, man, you probably want to kill me. Why are you even here?

Renata: This is my house.

Chase: Your house? So are you the leader? Are you in charge? Are you going to torture me? Like with cigarettes?

Nate: That's not funny, Chase.

But you know what, Journal? We all started to laugh, even Renata. Maybe because we were so confused about what was happening. And because Chase wasn't acting mean or angry; he was acting like he didn't mind waking up with us one bit.

Chase: Dude, I need food.

Nate: We have eggs. And cereal.

Chase: Excellent. What kind of cereal?

Renata said Froot Loops. Chase made a face, not happy to hear it, but then he ate three huge bowls—half the box.

Chase: Get me some Lucky Charms, okay? That's my cereal.

He said it like he was planning to stick around a while even though it was Saturday and he could have totally just gone home. It confused us even more.

Nate: We want you to apologize to Renata.

Chase: Seriously?

Nate: Seriously.

I can't remember exactly what Chase said. He kind of mumbled something—not an apology, I know that—and then he lay back down on the cot, Journal, flat on his back again, and fell asleep instantly. With a smile on his face. Like he was happy to be right where he was.

It has completely worn me out, remembering this. I wish I could show what I'm writing to Nate and Renata and ask them if this is how they remember it too. I think Renata would say: yes that's how it was, but I'm not so sure about Nate. He was being so careful with everything and acting so concerned about Chase. He was in a different space than we were. He had been planning for something good to happen, something completely different from what did happen. Of course, that is true for all of us, but I think for Nate, it is the truest. I think he was the one who cared the most about how things turned out with Chase. I'm not exactly sure why. Myself, I was just trying to stay close to my friends and do whatever they needed me to do.

Seriously, I have to go to bed early. That's how tired writing about that night made me. And it is so hard to remember it exactly when mostly I just wanted to forget it. Forget what we did. It's confusing and scary. I need to close my eyes for a minute. I need to breathe deeply so that I can stay calm. My mom taught me how to do it. Why won't she visit me? It's been four whole days.

Nathaniel, Son of James

Journal
Day Sixteen of Captivity

Evening: It is time to speak of my second GreyMount, to honor the sister who carries within her a secret gift. I can tell you about this, Great She, because it has nothing to do with the pact. I can also tell you that my second Grey-Mount knows the secret that was exchanged between me and the Master on the long past night in the little room, the night that led to my eventual imprisonment, the place where I first put myself in danger out of compassion for the Master. Although in truth, I did not tell my second GreyMount. I did not tell either of my GreyMounts what had happened in the little room. I had sworn on my honor that I would tell no one, and I never break a promise.

I first learned of my true sister's gift last spring, one afternoon after the terrors of the Great Hall were finished for the day. I was sitting between both sisters in the blue bedroom at the House of Glass and Magic, sitting up on the great bed in the sleeping chamber of my second sister, her mattress the size of a small room, the headboard nearly to the ceiling. Enough room for us all to rest together, which we sometimes did, without touching each other, as we all preferred. We were all three very tired that day, weary from a long and treacherous afternoon. My smaller sister was especially spent because it had been a day of persecution at the hand of the Master, who along with his soldiers had followed her through the Great Hall's many dim passageways, tormenting her with special ferocity. Her eyes were closed, but tears had formed beneath her eyelids and were moving slowly down her cheeks. And I remember that she was telling us that she couldn't stand any more cruelty in the Great Hall. That she would soon put an end to her time there, for the sake of her own survival.

The words cut me like a knife, Great She. And my first GreyMount, also with many tears said, "Please don't say that, Sister, or I will surely die."

That day I said, "This has gone on long enough. We must approach your tormentor."

My first GreyMount, her face full of doubt said, "What are you talking about? He won't listen to us."

I insisted that he would listen to me.

Then my first GreyMount spoke angrily. "Why will he listen to you? He doesn't have to listen to anybody! And why is he doing this to her in the first place? You said you knew, but you never explained it. When are you going to tell us?"

And I said, "I swore on my honor, Sister, that I would not talk about what happened in the past between myself and the Master."

My first GreyMount's face darkened into a thundercloud, but she kept silent, as she had been more and more silent during those weeks, full of rage and helplessness.

The smaller sister had not yet opened her eyes. She seemed almost asleep, breathing lightly, until she spoke in a voice that was heavy with the weight of the gift of knowing-without-being-told. She said, "You know something about Chase, don't you? Something that he did. Something no one else knows. Something he told you before I even came here."

I said nothing, astonished.

My first GreyMount asked accusingly, "Did you tell Renata what happened, but you refused to tell me?"

"He didn't tell me anything," the smaller GreyMount said, and it was true. She added softly, "I just know it. I saw it in my mind. A picture of the two of you, talking. Long ago."

"Do you know what was said?" I asked fearfully.

"No," she said. "But I know that it was something very, very important. Something that binds you to him."

It was the first time she revealed her gift to us, Great She. My first GreyMount again expressed confusion and uncertainty. But something in the voice of my second GreyMount made me believe that she truly had seen something in her mind, something that involved that long ago conversation with the Master.

Finally my first GreyMount asked, "Can you tell us more about what you saw, Sister?"

She closed her eyes again. "It's hard to explain," she said. "I'm afraid you won't believe me."

"Don't be afraid," my first GreyMount said. "Just tell us a little more."

"Sometimes I see things that have already happened," she told us. "I get impressions and I hear voices. But it's kind of a jumble. It can be very noisy and confusing." She closed her eyes again. "Please tell me that you believe me."

And we told her that we did believe her. Later, after my first GreyMount had left us, I asked my smaller sister again if she knew the Master's secret. And she said no. She did not know at that time. Nor did she know my secret. I was reassured then, that only the Master knew my terrible secret. And only I knew his. Still, I was gladdened to know of my smaller Grey-Mount's gift. Knowing that such a gift was part of our alliance gave me the courage that I had lacked in my Year of Watchfulness. The courage I needed to face the Master. With her help, I could match him on any battlefield without armies or weapons. I could also change the path of destruction that he was on; I could halt the slow spiraling of his life; I could rewrite his history as well as my own. All of this I could do, even as I rescued my beloved second GreyMount from the public torment she had borne and which had weighed so heavily upon our hearts.

. . .

How did she come to us at the moment when we most needed her? It was in the fall, after we had been banished from our false friends in the Great Halls of North Holmes. She came to us and enchanted us with her artistry. She brought us to the House of Glass and Magic, bound our wounds and fed us well and there we recovered and grew strong in friendship. She was also recovering, Great She—she had traveled far from the southern regions with her invisible parents—both of whom refuse to acknowledge her artistic genius, which she shared with us so generously. She told us in the early days of our togetherness that never had she known such friendship as ours and we believed her. We were more than happy to befriend her, as we had been most cruelly cast aside by our old comrades.

She was from distant regions, the southern lowlands, and had lived since birth under the great shadow cast by her mother, a woman of renown and dominion, who had prospered in her research into animal lore, magic totems, and dream language. Her art has a special name and it is full of mystery. In the lowlands she is known far and wide as Magdalena and even her daughter calls her Magdalena, rather than Mother. I first met Magdalena at the House of Glass and Magic and I was immediately aware of her power. It radiated from her hair and her silver adornments on her hands, which on that day were stained blue, the color of memory. My smaller Grey-Mount both loves and fears her mother, Great She, for she recognized her power as the same power stirring within herself.

She is, like me, an agent of watchfulness, and in this regard she is different from my first GreyMount, who is without guile and who will speak the truth always and without hesitation. Yet my new GreyMount shared with her sister a longing for human kindness and true friend-ship. This we offered her, and provided daily, although my first GreyMount and I had earlier embraced our shared isolation. We were alone, Great She, even during the time when it appeared we had many friends. Even before I chose her, I saw that my first sister moved through the Great Halls in regal solitude, keeping a solemn distance from all who would distract or diminish her, holding her head high.

Tonight I am filled with sadness for both my sisters because I am their leader and the place I have led them into is a place of defeat and loneliness. How can I serve them now? How can I comfort them and show thanks for their fealty? How will I give our suffering purpose in these dark times?

I replay these questions constantly and no clear answers come to me.

Renata's Journal

Social Worker

Tuesday, June 22

Martin Collier called early the next morning. "Given that it was my first visit to a teenager in prison," he reported gravely, "I think it went pretty well."

"It's not a prison, Martin."

"Right, right, right—detention."

"How did she seem to you?"

"Sad, actually. Forlorn. Needs a haircut. And way too thin."

"She is quite thin," Greta agreed. "She hates the food in here, and I can't blame her. Although for most of the other kids, detention meals are a big improvement over their usual diet."

"I suppose. But to see Renata . . ."

"We're watching her, Martin, don't worry. The staff seems to think she's doing better. Was she surprised that you came to visit her?"

"She was. But not in a suspicious way, more like she couldn't believe I would take the time. I told her that I was there because I was sorry I hadn't done more to protect her in the hallway. It felt good to tell her that, Greta, it really did."

"Did she say anything about . . . the actual night of the kidnapping?"

"Not really. I started by asking her if she was worried about her upcoming hearings. She said no. She said she knows her parents will get her off the hook. That's the term she used, 'off the hook.' She was calling her parents by their first names—Magdalena and Stefano—so at first I didn't know who she was talking about. She almost sounded as though they had all been through this before. Is that possible?"

"She has no criminal record, if that's what you mean. She may have been referring to a pattern in her relationship with her parents. I've only met the mother. She seemed very . . . unsympathetic."

"Well . . . here's the part I thought you should know. Renata told me that this whole mess was her fault. I asked her if she meant because she was the one Chase went after at school, and she shook her head no. She said that none of this would have happened if she hadn't brought her own bad luck with her to North Holmes. That's pretty much a direct quote."

Greta contemplated this for a moment. "That is odd. Neither Nate nor Katie have ever spoken as though they blame her in any way."

"She seems to be blaming herself. Last night she seemed . . . how should I say it . . . burdened with guilt. That was my impression."

"Hmmm. I'll meet with her tomorrow and see if she'll say more about feeling guilty. Meanwhile, Could you visit her again? It appears she's willing to confide in you, which could really help me—especially with her court date so soon. She might very well tell you more than she's told anyone else, including me."

"I'll be happy to do that."

"One more favor—it's about Chase. I'm afraid I need to see him in person. To actually see his face. Is there any way that you could help make that happen?"

"That will be more complicated. But let me make a few phone calls to some other coaches. I'll see what I can do."

Katie Havenga's Journal for Mrs. Shield

Tuesday, June 22—Evening Personal Time

Hi Mrs. Shield, I know you told me I don't need to write about what happens here in juvie anymore, but remember how we had a fire drill on Monday? I wanted to tell you that the fire drill was just awful for me. I was sitting in the day room and then Lee Ann got the word on the intercom and we had to all get up and get in a line and then Lee Ann put on an orange vest and then we all walked single file down the hallway to the gym and then outside, and it turns out we were the last pod and the other pods were already outside, standing in their lines.

Then I saw my friends, Mrs. Shield.

I haven't seen my friends since intake. It was the strangest, hardest thing, because I couldn't go over to them or talk to them or do anything like I normally would, like when I would see them at school. All I could do was look at them.

First I looked at Nate and he saw me and he smiled at me—he has such a beautiful smile—my mom always said he smiles like an angel. He was holding himself really tall and stiff, like a soldier, like he wanted me to see that he was still himself, still strong, still Nate. And even in those ugly green sweats, he looked really, really handsome, except that his hair is getting way too long in the front—it almost covers his eyes. I wanted to tell him he shouldn't hide his eyes, because they are so blue and pretty, but then I remembered that we are in juvie and no one cares how pretty your eyes are in juvie. Nobody looks good in here. I wondered what he was thinking when he looked at me. I know I look really bad. My hair is hopeless without mousse, and my skin isn't so great right now because I don't have my special products, and I haven't gotten much sunshine, and I'm white as a ghost. Actually, I'm the color of Nate. So there we were in the yard, looking at each other like we were starving to see each other, and knowing that we are both having a rough time in here. That was hard, Mrs. Shield.

And then I turned to the other side of the yard, and there was Renata. She was standing kind of back from the boys in her pod and she was holding a large black book, which was strange, because in my pod we were told not to take anything outside with us for the fire drill. I think her pod supervisor might have even come over to her and said something about it, but he didn't seem mad and she just nodded up at him and didn't seem upset and she let him take it away from her. She looked so small. She is even smaller than some of the little boys in her pod. But when she saw me, she smiled too, but it wasn't like a secret-message smile, it was more just a pure smile. Like she was so happy just to see me. Just to lay eyes on me. And you know what was strange? She didn't look terrible. Her sweats were too big, and her hair is growing out kind of strangely but there was something about how she was smiling—she looked okay. Renata—okay in juvie! And I was so glad that we could see each other, just for a moment. I love her so much, Mrs. Shield. I don't think I could ever love another friend as much as I love her. Except of course, Nate.

Later the same day I was with my pod in the library, and the Youth Supervisor got a call on the intercom and found out it was a lockdown. We all had to get up and walk in a line back to our pods with Lee Ann, we had to walk in a line through the hallway, but then the boy pod was also coming through the hallway so the girl pod had to turn and face the wall and not look at the boy pod as they walked by. Except out of the corner of my eye I snuck one little look and I'm pretty sure I saw the back of Nate's head before he disappeared. Nobody else in here has hair like his, Mrs. Shield. It's almost white. It's ghost hair.

There is a new girl in my pod named Jackie who never talked to me before lockdown, but when we were outside she asked me if I was one of the kids who kidnapped Chase Dobson, like she had just found out about it and it made her all interested in me. I told her that I was, and it was the first time I ever said anything to anybody about it in here, except you. Her eyes got really big, like with admiration, and she said it was an honor to be in juvie with me. I am not exaggerating—she said HONOR.

I asked her how she knew Chase Dobson and she said everybody knows Chase Dobson. Then she said something really strange, Mrs. Shield. She said that it must have been hard for us not to kill him. I am serious, she really said that. And she wasn't kidding either, she was like completely serious. Then I got kind of scared. There are some tough girls in here, Mrs. Shield. I wonder if my mom ever worked with Jackie, which is completely possible because Mom works with all the messed up girls in this town. I am going to ask her if she knows Jackie. It will give us something to talk about besides me.

I guess all the girls in my pod know what I did now. Another girl asked me if it's true that the other kidnappers are here too. And so I told them yes and that my friend is stuck in the little boy's pod, and they all instantly knew who she was. Some of them have seen Renata. They said she's not friendly, and she never talks to anybody, not even the teachers, and all she does is draw in a notebook with a black cover, even during movies. I guess she has a nickname in here already and it is Rambo, like making fun of how small she is, which probably really hurts her feelings, like when Chase called her Rico. Plus I don't get how she can have time to draw and still do her homework and still write in her journal. Which brings me to my main point of today's journal writing, Mrs. Shield. I think it would be really good if you would let me see Renata. I think it would be the right thing to do since it isn't fair that she has to be stuck in Pod C with boys. If you don't want us to talk face-to-face, maybe you could ask if we could at least talk on the phone. I am really, really, really serious about this. I am begging you.

So anyway, there are three different girls in juvie right now who hate Chase Dobson, Mrs. Shield—me, Renata, and that Jackie girl. Maybe Nate hates him too, but I am not sure. There are some things I am not sure about with Nate. He was going to tell me some stuff that happened a long time ago, but then he never did. He told me some things, but he didn't tell me other things. At first I thought he told Renata because she knows more than me, but it's not because Nate told her. Somebody else told her. Actually, Chase told her. I think it's okay to tell you that. Because I don't know what he told her, exactly. Just like I don't know what Nate told her. Chase told her something because she told him something. It was on the last day that Chase was in her apartment. When everything got so strange. That's all I can say.

Mrs. Shield, I really appreciate all your help. Something is making me feel extra bad today and it's that my mom hasn't been here in a week—and she hasn't called me or written me a note or anything. She came once after that one big meltdown in the Visitor's Room that maybe you heard about, but she only stayed for a few minutes, and she was really calm, and she told me that she knew she needed to stop coming to juvie every day—she said that she had seen the light. I didn't argue with her because I was still recovering from how she went off on me the night before. I think I said, "Whatever, Mom," and I might have said it kind of cold, mainly because I didn't believe her—I figured she would show up again the next night.

But now it has been seven days without one single word from her and it is making me feel really bad. Like maybe she forgot about me or doesn't care about me. Is that crazy? Because I know that I was complaining about her in my journal, but now whenever I think about her, I feel sad. I miss her. And it's making me think about something, something that happened a long time ago to my mom, something I learned. But I can't tell you what it is because of the pact.

Can you believe it, Mrs. Shield? I miss my mom. If you see her, could you tell her that for me?

Social Worker

The Domestic Crisis Center was located ten miles south of the JDC, on the north side of Holland, Michigan. It was a sleek little building, cheerily landscaped with black-eyed Susans, mums, and beach grass. A brass plaque on the side of the automatic doors proclaimed "25 Years of Serving the Women of Odetta County." Inside, the reception room was tidy but welcoming, with a miniature table for children, stacked with cars, building blocks, and board books.

The social worker checked in with the receptionist, explaining that she had no appointment, but wanted to speak with Claire Havenga, if she was available. She waited ten minutes, flipping through a Weight Watchers magazine, and then Claire's head appeared from a side door to the reception area. "Is this about Katie?" she asked worriedly.

"No, Katie is fine, everything is fine. I actually wanted to talk to you about Nate today, if you don't mind. I thought it might be nice to see you away from the detention center."

"You're right. Come in, welcome."

Her office was at the end of the hallway, equally no-nonsense, but with a few touches of hominess—a vase filled with real daisies, a poster on the wall of two Hispanic girls embracing under a rainbow with the word: "Trust!" There was a framed photo of herself with a younger Katie—the two of them in kayaks, wearing life vests, matching pig tails, and broad smiles. "Can I get you anything, Greta? Coffee or tea?"

The social worker shook her head and sat in the chair beside Claire's desk—a complete role reversal. "We've noticed you've been staying away from the JDC this past week, Claire."

"I realized I wasn't helping Katie. And I was driving myself crazy, being in that place every day and not getting through to her."

"You do seem calmer."

"I have to be calm here. I can't be anybody's out-of-control mother here. My trips to the JDC were affecting my work, as I'm sure you can imagine."

"Sometimes life interferes."

Claire asked hesitantly, "Have you ever had something happen to you that made it impossible for you to do your job?"

Greta nodded. "When I was going through my divorce, I became a robot. I always showed up. I never missed a day. I met with my kids. I went to every single staff meeting. But I wasn't really there. I wasn't available. For almost a whole year, to be honest."

The two women stared at each other a long moment. "Thank you for telling me that," Claire said finally.

"They brought me out of it, actually. Nate and Katie and Renata. This case is so strange and challenging."

"Why do you say that?"

"These are definitely not kids who would ordinarily be in juvenile detention. But none of them will tell me what really happened. I'm used to secrecy, defensiveness—all of those things in detained teenagers—but this is different. I find myself actually admiring them, admiring their resolve and their loyalty to one another, even as I'm working so hard to unravel it. I've been thinking a lot about your daughter. How deeply she loves her friends. She's loyal beyond her years. Nate calls her a noble warrior. He's a bit of a budding fantasy writer, did you know that?"

Claire smiled. "I know he loves to write. Katie brings his stories home, but she won't let me read them. She says he'll be famous someday."

"He won't let me help him. I was wondering if you would mind if we talked about him a little bit. If you could tell me what you know about him, as the mother of his closest friend."

"I would do anything to help Nate. But the truth is, I really don't know very much about him. He's always charming with me and seems like such a gentle soul, but I've never heard him say anything about his home life, or about the fact that his father lives so far away. He never mentions either of his parents or his brothers. Or his sister. Almost like they don't exist. I remember asking Katie about it and she told me that Nate didn't like to talk about his family."

"Do you have any sense of why?"

"I suspect Nate is hiding something painful. I'm used to just accepting this sort of thing because of my work—I didn't worry about it. I thought he might be gay. Katie says no. So then I just assumed he was in a lot of pain about his father. The man moved away some years ago, as I'm sure you know. I don't think there's been any contact between them at all. And that would be hard for a sensitive boy like Nate. Maybe even harder than Katie's experience of never having known her father."

The social worker was startled to hear Claire mention Katie's father. She took it as an invitation and pretended to be a bit surprised. "Your daughter has never met her father?"

"Never. Has she said anything to you about it?"

"If she had, it would be confidential. But no, she hasn't. Is her father in the area?"

"I honestly don't know."

"Do you know if he's alive?"

"He could be alive. I just . . . I never kept up any sort of contact with him."

"So Katie doesn't ask you for information about him?"

"A few times when she was younger. I tried to be as honest as I could be. I told her there wasn't much to tell. I told her there was never any sort of relationship. Which gets back to my point about Nate. I think having your father leave you is harder than never having known your father."

A pause. "Claire, I know we were going to talk about Nate, but since you've brought up Katie's father, I would like to ask you a little bit more about him. And about how much Katie knows about him."

Claire's face grew more troubled. "Why do we need to talk about him? What does it have do with the case if Katie hasn't brought it up?"

"I'm trying to figure out how likely it is that Katie knows about...what happened between you and her father."

"I told you...she knows nothing," Claire insisted. Then her eyes widened in distress. "Oh my God," she exclaimed softly, "what do *you* know?"

"What do you think I know?"

"Who have you talked to? What have you heard?"

The social worker said in a rush, "I heard that you were raped as a teenager."

Claire put her hands to the sides of her head, as though trying to block this information from her ears. Then she uncovered her ears and asked pleadingly, "Please don't tell me that it was Katie who told you that."

"It wasn't Katie."

A sigh of relief. "Thank God."

"It was Lenora Dobson."

Claire gasped. "Of course. Lenora Dobson. When did you talk to her?"

"I met with her recently to discuss the case. She told me that long ago you announced at a committee meeting that your pregnancy was the result of a rape. Do you remember telling her that?"

"Yes. Yes, I remember. When I was younger, I used to sometimes tell people . . . what had happened. It was a personal thing with me. I didn't want to be ashamed of it because it hadn't been my fault. And I was pretty far along when I figured out that I was pregnant. There was no fixing it, if you know what I mean. Then afterward, I was just so grateful for Katie. She was just the greatest little kid a mom could have from day one. And through the years, as she got older, I just had to hope that people in town wouldn't remember the days when I used to . . . bring it up."

"It appears that Lenora Dobson is a woman who never forgets."

"I know that. It actually came up rather recently between us as well. Last year. She brought it up hoping it would shut me up about another girl Chase had harassed at the junior high. A shy little girl named Della."

"Nate mentioned Della in his journal!" Greta exclaimed softly.

"I wanted approach the school with legal charges, but the girl eventually backed down. Her parents transferred her to another school. Lenora probably thought that I dropped the ball out of fear." She paused, thinking. "Greta, why did my past come up at all between you and Lenora? Was Lenora implying that it had something to do with the case?"

"I think . . . for Lenora . . . it was a possible explanation for why Katie would do something so . . . extreme."

"Like kidnap her poor innocent son? Because of course the real criminal must be Katie."

"I'm afraid that is what she was implying, Claire."

"Oh my God, that bully! I work with girls, Greta. They tell me things. I've had a few come through here and tell me their Chase Dobson stories. You'd be surprised what I know." She glanced fretfully at the clock on her desk. "I have a young client coming in very soon," she said. "And we've hardly spoken about Nate."

"We'll talk another time about Nate. What we did talk about was perhaps more important."

"Greta . . . you said Katie didn't tell you, but do you think she knows? I've tried so hard to protect her."

"I honestly don't know. She hasn't mentioned it."

"We should definitely talk again soon. But I'm going to continue to stay away from the detention center. I think it's for the best. If Katie says anything to you about missing me, the slightest thing, can you let me know? I'd be there in a heartbeat, if I thought she needed me."

The social worker promised to do this.

First GreyMount Katie

Journal Entry Wednesday, June 23—Morning Break

Oh God, he wouldn't leave, Journal. We just couldn't get him to leave. First he said he thought it would be awesome to spend another night at Renata's and have nobody know where he was, and then on Sunday there was something on the local news about him being missing, but when we told him about it, he wasn't upset, he was excited! Monday was Memorial Day and there was no school and we could hardly get him out of bed. Then it was Tuesday and when we got to school, everybody was talking about Chase Dobson getting kidnapped and we all just kept really quiet because we were sure he would go home that day and be gone when we went to Renata's. But after school, there he was—sound asleep on his futon—still there!

And the headline of the *Tribune* that day was: "MISSING ATHELETE SPARKS LOCAL SEARCH," which we made the mistake of showing to him—he was thrilled! The article had a picture of the soccer team with his face circled in red and the article said that his parents were frantic because he had mysteriously disappeared from a beach party. Then Chase wanted to watch himself again on the local news, and he told Nate to bring a laptop into the laundry room so that he could keep up with the developments about his disappearance. Sure enough the local news was playing stories about it, saying that a promising young athlete had disappeared with an unidentified male from an unsupervised party and foul play was suspected and school officials were cooperating and the police were working with the family who were well known in the community, blah, blah, blah.

Journal, he LOVED it! He loved every minute of it. He set up the laptop in front of this big chair, and he gave Renata a list of all his favorite junk food, and he finally took a shower in the little bathroom in the laundry room, and Nate brought him some clean clothes, and then Chase basically did nothing but watch news reports about himself for the next two days. He said he was on vacation. That's what he called it, Journal. HIS VACATION!

He knew that we were getting more and more confused that he didn't want to go home, and he was getting a big kick out of that too. He thought it was hilarious. He called me "Warden Girl" and he called Nate "Sheriff

Wilson." And he would see all these people talking about him on the afternoon and evening news—coaches, teachers, teammates—telling the reporters what a great jock he was and how they were so worried about him. He would recline his big old chair and drink from his flask and talk back to the screen like it was a person. We listened to him having a great time in the laundry room and tried to figure out what we should do. Should we call his parents? Should we call the police? Should I at least tell my mom? Should we offer to give him money if he would just please leave?

I couldn't tell my mom. I went home for a little while the Saturday before and got in a big fight with her because I was buying cereal she didn't approve of (for Chase). Then on Sunday I told her that we were all working on special projects for U.S. History so that she wouldn't mind me sleeping over again at Renata's. I told her our report was on the Civil War. It was probably the most complicated lie I had ever told my mom and it just kept mushrooming into other details. When I went home again late on Monday because I needed clean clothes and I also needed to ride my bike to the store and get more food for Chase, I found out that my mom had actually gone out and gotten me three library books about the Civil War, trying to be helpful, and she told me she missed me and asked me a million questions, including had I heard about Chase Dobson getting kidnapped Friday. When she asked me that, I acted like I hadn't heard about it because I was so busy with my Civil War report. Then instead of doing my real homework, I went into my room and fell asleep in my own bed and I slept until 8 o'clock that night and then my mom woke me up and said that Nate had called me three times while I was sleeping.

Mom: I think it's something about the report, big girl.

Me: Oh yeah? What did he say?

Mom: He said he needs to talk to you about the prisoner of war situation. Would you like a sandwich after you talk to him? You never had any dinner. What did you eat all weekend?

Nate: [On the phone] Can you go to the store again? I know it's late, but can you please go to the store? Chase is getting really hungry and he wants Hot Pockets. He's completely insane tonight.

Me: Tell him to go home.

Nate: He wants more Xanax. Should I get him some? He's acting desperate.

Me: Tell him you'll give him the Xanax if he goes home.

Nate: Can you please just come over and help us? He's being completely unreasonable.

Me: Nate, since when is Chase reasonable?

Nate: Could you just please get the food and come over here? Once you're here I'll go get the Xanax. I don't want to leave Renata alone with him.

Then I had to make up a long involved excuse for why I needed to go back to Renata's and work some more on the Civil War report and take all the supplies she bought me in a backpack and spend the night at Renata's and take the project to school the next day because that's when the project was due. A bunch of crap! Before I left the house, I took money out of her purse for Chase's Hot Pockets.

I pretty much lied to my mom 24/7 for that entire week. The lies got bigger and wilder; they were piling up like bodies at the end of the Civil War. No wonder she has stopped visiting me in juvie, Journal. No wonder she cries every time she looks at me. I can't believe how many lies I told her. I am the worst daughter in the world.

. . .

By Wednesday we knew something serious was wrong with Chase. He was falling apart. He looked like a homeless person in Nate's old clothes, and he refused to take another shower, and he ate constantly, but only really bad snack food. He drank from his flask all day, which by then I knew was vodka—he wasn't even bothering to mix it with Gatorade anymore. I think Nate gave him a lot of Xanax, but he still wouldn't go home. He stayed in the room and sat in the recliner and watched ESPN and the local news. Sometimes he would lift his flask and toast the screen. "Here's to all the games North Holmes will lose without me next year!" he would say, and then he would laugh his insane laugh. And whenever they showed his family on the news—which they did several times a day after the Tuesday headlines—that was when he laughed the loudest. I mean people were looking for him and saying really nice things about him and once they showed a picture of his little sister breaking down in tears and it was like it didn't mean ANYTHING to him.

Nate tried to talk to him.

> Nate: *You have to call somebody. They're starting to think something really bad happened to you. Really bad. Like they're searching for your body.*

> Chase: *Let them search. It will bring some excitement to their boring lives.*

> Nate: *Chase, what if somebody remembers seeing me at that party and the police think I'm the one who did something to you?*

> Chase: *You did do something to me, Sheriff Wilson. Ha ha ha. You kidnapped me, remember? Haven't you been watching the news?*

> Nate: *I know you're mad at your family, but how long are you going to keep this going? You can't just stay here. It's not a good idea.*

> Chase: *It is a good idea. I like being here. My girls are*

*taking good care of me. Except Warden Girl has
a bad attitude. Tell her she needs to smile more.
Ha ha ha.*

Nate: *You have to stop with the vodka. And I'm not
giving you any more Xanax. You're scaring me.
You really have a problem and I don't know how
to help you.*

Chase would laugh at Nate for worrying and keep
drinking. Two or three times a day, he took a nap. Nate
said it was the pills, wiping him out.

Renata tried to talk to him too. She got it into her
head that they had something in common. I heard them
from Renata's kitchen, talking in low voices; I couldn't
hear what they were saying, but I knew it was intense. I
never tried to talk to him, Journal, I never once did that.
I couldn't stand to be in the same room with him, I swear
I couldn't—it always made me feel kind of sick to even
make eye contact with him. Nate still wanted to help him,
and now Renata felt sorry for him, but I knew he wouldn't
take any help from kids like us. Or be our friend. I don't
think anybody could be Chase's friend. I just brought him
food and tried to ignore his mean remarks and his laughing. I slept over at Renata's every night he was there so
she wouldn't have to be alone with him. She was acting
like she wasn't afraid of him anymore and this scared me
more than anything. Somehow he had gotten to her the
same way he got to Nate. By the fourth day, we were in

so deep, Journal. I knew we were really, really in trouble. I should have gone home, and told my mom everything. But something kept me there, kept me part of it, kept me waiting for Chase to go and take his big secret with him.

Except that now I know that even though I never learned what Chase's secret was, I'm still burdened by it. I'm trapped underneath it. Even though I don't know what it is. Does that make any sense, Journal?

I remember this one time after I watched Renata bringing Chase his cereal, I asked her how she could stand to do even the slightest little thing for him after what he did to her, and she said, "I'm just holding on, same as you, Katie. He says he's leaving tomorrow. I believe him. Then all of this will be over." But her voice, when she said this, was really defeated and sad. Because she was having doubts. She knew we were in big trouble. She knew.

I have to write about one more thing, Journal, and I've been putting it off and it's really painful, almost as painful as my secret, even though I know that no one will ever see this notebook but me.

It's about the drugs, the drugs we got for Chase. It's better if I write it down, confessing my sins, which I know about because my mom was raised Catholic, except now she calls herself a recovering Catholic. Because ever since I was a little kid I promised my mom that I would never touch drugs. And, Journal, I never have, not even once. Well once I tasted a beer at a slumber party but I HATED it. But I have never once used actual drugs, Journal. I would NEVER smoke pot and so this part of the story of what happened makes me feel sick to my stomach while I am writing it. Because one of the true facts about what happened is that when Chase begged us for drugs, we gave them to him. Nate gave him the Xanax and the Adderall and Renata gave him her mom's Oxycontin. And I brought him the vodka. We were all guilty. The police said we forced him to take drugs against his will and that part isn't true, but we gave him everything he asked for. Why did we do that? Why did we feel like we couldn't say no to him? Even me, the one who hated him the most—I just couldn't just say no. It just felt so completely out of our control. He was Chase Dobson. He was king of our school.

Don't even ask me how I got the vodka. It has to do with my mom and a really weird older guy that I know, and telling lie after lie, and if I even attempt to write it down I will cry a river of tears.

When we found out that both Nate and Renata were giving him pills at the same time and it still wasn't enough, that was when we told him that we were done. We wouldn't give him any more of anything and his vacation was over and he had to go home. And then he turned into the old Chase, Journal. He told us what he was going to do to us if we ever said one word about how he refused to leave and made us bring him pills and alcohol. He talked to us one at a time on that last night, and he told us what he was going to reveal about us. Unless we promised him that we wouldn't tell anyone the way it had really happened. We had to let him tell it his way. We all agreed. That was our pact. It was one of the few things we agreed about that last terrible day.

We just wanted him to go home! We wanted it to end. And I wanted never ever to lay eyes on him again. Every day in juvie I tell myself I will never have to see Chase Dobson III ever again, and I will never have to bring him food, or steal vodka for him, or hear his insane laughing when he saw himself on the news. No matter how bad it is in here, at least I will never have to do any of those things ever again. And that is comforting to me, it really is, even in this place, Journal, even locked up like a criminal in juvie.

Social Worker

Thursday, June 24

This time, it was Katie's journal that the social worker opened first. She was instantly, almost unbearably disappointed. Again, there were very few pages—five since the last time she had read the journals. She scanned the hastily scrawled, barely legible entries and found not a single mention of the past, the crime, the events leading up to the kidnapping. She had been clinging to her belief that this no-nonsense girl was the most likely to deliver a coherent narrative, perhaps even something that would give significance to whatever riddles and ciphers she expected to find in the other two journals. But she was wrong again. She pushed herself backward in her rolling chair and lowered her head into her arms and groaned, struggling to contain her aggravation.

Then she tried again, lowering her face to the notebook and scanning Katie's five new pages. There was a paragraph about a resident named Jackie Marquez, a bright but self-destructive girl who had been in detention twice before. Another plaintive request for permission to see Renata. The final page included a few lines about missing her mother—and at this the social worker smiled and, despite her frustration, wrote *Tell Claire* on a sticky note and attached it to the top of her desk.

The social worker closed Katie's journal, set it aside, and opened Nate's, flipping to his new writings, forcing herself to plow through the first several paragraphs of his now familiar, overblown style, typing notes into her computer as she read.

NATE/NOTES:
June 24
From Nate's journal:
   Believes that his father is never coming back—why?
   James Wilson an architect in Cleveland?
   Nate his father's favorite?
   Nate fascinated by the Dobson family's athleticism.
   Very bitter toward sister—call her again.

Impulsively, the social worker picked up her phone and dialed the Wilson household. A child answered on the first ring. "Is Natalie there?" the social worker asked.

The phone clattered to the floor, but a few minutes later, Natalie's hopeful voice came on the line. "Is this about the used dishwasher?"

"This is Greta Shield, Natalie. Nate's social worker, remember?"

Natalie's voice flattened. "I don't have anything new to tell you."

"I have something to ask you. Can I just speak to you for one minute?"

"Not here," Natalie said. "I'll call you back on my cell." She hung up, but called back immediately. "I'm in the garage," she explained.

"Why do you need to call me from the garage?"

"I told you, Mrs. Shield, my mom doesn't want me to talk to anybody from juvie."

"I'm very sorry to hear that she still feels that way, Natalie. I'm really trying to help your brother."

"I don't think she cares about him anymore. I don't think she even wants him to live here once he gets out. Do you know when that's going to be? People keep asking."

"Who is asking?"

"People at my church. Bible study friends. And some guy keeps calling over here and asking me when Nate is getting out, but he won't leave his name."

From the phone, she heard a child's distant voice, calling Natalie. Followed by a wail: *I can't open it!*

"I have to go," Natalie said. "I'm babysitting."

"I need to quickly ask you something about your father.

Nate says he is never coming back to North Holmes. Is that your impression too?"

Natalie's voice dropped, she was almost whispering, "He's not allowed to come back to North Holmes."

"Not allowed? By whom?"

"Mom." Then she added, "Nobody knows. You can't tell anybody this. It's like one of those things where you can't come near another person."

"Do you mean a restraining order?"

"Yeah, that's it. But it's not for my mom. It's for us kids."

The social worker kept her voice calm, "And why is that, Natalie? What did your father do?"

"You want to hear something weird?" Natalie asked. "I don't know what he did. Nobody ever told me."

"Do you think Nate knows what he did?"

"If he did he wouldn't tell me. He doesn't talk to me. Except to insult my faith. Constantly, Mrs. Shield. Like every chance he gets."

There was a crash in the garage and a child began to wail. Then another child, yelling for Natalie. "I hafta go," Natalie said and she hung up.

. . .

The social worker put Nate's journal aside and opened Renata's sketchpad to find two new drawings. One was a drawing of Martin's visit and the second was a drawing of the three suspects and Chase, in what she recognized to be Renata's apartment, surrounded by churning water. On the surface of the water floated many bottles and pills. It was a scene of chaos and desperation. She went back to the drawing of Martin and was all the more unsettled to see that Renata had included her own image through a window of the visiting room, herself peering out, watching over the interaction between Martin and Renata. She suspected from this that Renata knew they were working together. This was jarring, given Nate's suggestion that Renata had some sort of psychic gift. The social worker picked up the phone again and dialed the coach's number.

"This is going to sound strange," she began, "but when you visited Renata, did you mention that you knew me?"

"Of course not. You said you didn't want her to know we were working together."

"Is it remotely possible that you just let some detail or other slip about how you've spoken to me?"

"No, Greta. There was absolutely no reason to bring that up."

"Okay. All right. I believe you, Martin, and forgive me if I sound accusing, but there's a new twist surfacing in this case—actually several new twists based on the journals—and right now I'm trying to decipher Renata's latest drawings."

"Would you like me to take a look at them?"

"Maybe just one in particular. Can you stop by the detention center later this afternoon?"

"I can come around five if that's okay.

"Five is fine. I'll be working late anyway."

"I was actually planning that second visit to Renata tonight."

"I really want to show you this drawing before your visit. See you at five—come in the north doors and security will bring you back to my office."

"See you then."

Greta felt a pang of disloyalty then, because she always promised her residents that their journals were confidential. But she simply had to show the coach how Renata had portrayed him.

She glanced at her clock. It was 3:30. The day had flown by. She had hoped to meet individually with Katie, Nate, and Renata, but she'd spent far too much time poring over their encoded journals, especially Nate's. She decided she would confront them one at a time, starting first thing the next morning.

* * *

When Martin saw the drawing he emitted a low exclamation of surprise. "I never told her anything about our connection, Greta. How could she have known?"

"I don't know. Nate thinks that she has some kind of psychic ability. He calls it 'the gift of not needing to be told.' Take a look at the page where he talks about it." She flipped through the journal and found the page, holding it in front of him.

213

He scanned the page curiously. "Good Lord, look at his handwriting!" he exclaimed. "How can you even read this?" He began to read aloud: " 'I swore on my honor that I would not talk about myself and the Master.' Who is he talking about?"

"The Master is Chase."

"*What?* Why is he calling Chase his master?"

Abruptly Greta took the notebook back and shut it. The coach was waiting for a reply. "Because Chase is powerful at school," Greta said. "And because he was at one time . . . important to Nate."

"Greta, if you have reason to believe that the two boys were friends before the kidnapping, you should share this information with their lawyers."

"I know. And I will. But first . . . first there are still some pieces of the puzzle I don't have yet. I want to be sure that I know everything there is to know about my kids before I talk to their lawyers again."

"Greta, you keep calling them *my kids*."

"Well . . . they are my kids, Martin. My responsibilities."

"Listen, can I share something with you? Something my wife told me? Kathy said you have kind of a reputation for working late, working on weekends, never taking vacations. I'm just saying that maybe you're getting a little too emotionally involved. Maybe you need to get some distance."

A pause. "Like the distance you kept from the girls who were bullied by Chase Dobson outside your classroom?" she asked.

"That's . . . that's not fair, Greta. I've told you I regret not helping Renata; I've admitted it."

"Well, I admit that I don't have your skill at keeping distance. I want to get to the bottom of this case. I have exactly one week left. Are you willing to help me or not?"

"I've already said I would help you. But I don't believe in ESP or whatever you call it. Renata must have figured out that we know each other some other way."

Not possible, Greta thought, but aloud she asked, "Will you call me tomorrow? Tell me if you learn anything new?"

"Of course," he said. But there was now a chill in his voice.

# Nathaniel, Son of James

Journal
Day Eighteen of Captivity

Evening: Tonight I am reduced to writing on a single ragged sheet from a yellow pad that I begged the Prison Steward to give me. I have no other paper, Great She, for I offered my bound writings up to you earlier today and you have not yet called for me to tell me if you are pleased with my newest revelations. This has sorely troubled me in the fading hours of the eighteenth day of my imprisonment, and I have told my steward that I am unable to participate in the games of the evening and that instead I seek solitude and rest for my sore body and my overburdened soul. He said to me, in a voice that held neither sympathy nor appreciation, "You might feel a whole lot better if you'd get off your butt and get some exercise."

He was referring to the challenges of the games, for he does not understand the darkness and menace that exist at the heart of the game for me. He does not appreciate the superior pursuits of the pen and the well-turned phrase. Still he agreed to let me remain alone in a state of confinement, free to unburden myself to you. I am anxious to hear from you and fear that I will not sleep well this night, nor any night until I have received your acknowledgments of my efforts. Did I not share my sadness regarding my noble father? And did I not admit my unease at having to even mention my shadow-sister—even to spend a few hours describing the affliction of family that she represents?

Perhaps you think that I went too far in ascribing my true sister with the gift of knowing-without-having-to-be-told? Perhaps you are a non-believer in powers such as those of my true sister? Perhaps you are less sure now about other revelations that I have shared, such as those about my first GreyMount, or my mother the Shadow Wraith, or The Master? In the hours since I gave my journal to my Leader to present to you, I have felt with greater and greater urgency the need to convince you, Great She, for I have tried to speak the truth as much as possible without betraying my sacred vows. Indeed, I am near despair as I write this now, pained to be writing on yellow scratch-pad paper; I am unable to control my calligraphy and the speed with which my thoughts pour onto this ignoble page.

I know that you have tried with great resolve to help me and to help my sisters. You have shown me kindness and consideration in the days since I arrived at the Place of Contrition. Perhaps I am becoming less and less capable of enduring all that I have endured, especially in the third week of captivity, during which there have been many incidents that have shaken my resolve, including lockdown and resident search, during which I could think only of my sisters, wondering if they were also enduring these trials. Perhaps it is becoming too painful for me to think of what my path has cost them. In truth, I am weary, Great She.

Last night I said that my father had not turned from me, but that was not true, not true, not true, not true! My father has turned from me! He who once was with me, cannot ever again be with me—he has left me. My sister, with her Book of Nightmares, her righteousness, and her obedience to the Queen of Shadows, does not know why he left. My small brothers in their innocence and their blindness do not know why he left. My GreyMounts do not know why. The Queen knows why he is gone, although she lies about him and does not know that I have seen the truth with my own eyes.

Only the Master knows all of it. Only the Master holds my secret close against his bloody heart as I hold his.

Tonight I feel the hot breath of doom around me. There is no way out of this place. I must prepare myself to stay here for a long time, a long time—beyond the summer, into the fall, maybe a whole year, I don't know, I don't know anymore. I only know that I am doomed, Great She. I cannot tell you what really happened. Please do not be angry with me. Please do not turn from me. Please do not turn from my sisters—they are innocent! Please don't ask us to betray the pact. Please, please, don't abandon me, I cannot bear another terrible absence.

Katie Havenga's Journal for Mrs. Shield

Journal Entry Friday, June 25—Morning Break Time
Hi, Mrs. Shield, I just wanted to write a few more pages
for you in case you are mad that I didn't write enough
before you collected the journals yesterday. I've been
so busy with homework and plus my mind is kind of
occupied with wondering why my mom doesn't visit
me anymore, and I am actually kind of really worried
about that. Have you heard anything? Have you had
a chance to talk to her? I am sorry if you think that I
wrote too much again about life in juvie after you told
me not to, but I had some really important things to
tell you, especially about Lucille who is in my pod and
who is acting like she's my best friend and being super
nice to me and it is making me feel kind of nervous

because she thinks I'm really, really tough, like her, but actually I'm not—I'm mostly really sorry about what I did and also pretty scared about being stuck in here for the rest of the summer and I just really miss my friends and I miss my mom so much and I don't want you to be mad at me, but you haven't talked to me in SO LONG!

Are you mad at me, Mrs. Shield? I don't think I can handle it if you are mad at me. I think I must be having a really bad day. I think I might be losing my mind. I am freaked out because yesterday somebody (I can't tell you who) told me that when we get out, we should get revenge on Chase Dobson together and that she knows some guys who could help us. That scared me so much. I am not a criminal. I am just not into the revenge thing, Mrs. Shield. When I get out of here I am going to never even look at Chase Dobson again and hopefully never think about him. I will never get in any kind of trouble and I will never lie to my mom about anything important. Ever, ever AGAIN! This is the worst thing that has ever happened to me in my entire life and I can't believe how bad things are right now and I can't believe that I might have to wait a really long time before I'm free.

I miss my mom. I don't know if I can take it anymore, Mrs. Shield. Please, please, please don't be mad at me.

P. S.: Mrs. Shield, the secret that Chase Dobson knows about me would just like really, really destroy my mom if people knew. That's why I can't tell you. That's why I have to go along with his story. That's all I can say, okay? Please don't be mad at me!

First GreyMount Katie

Journal Entry Friday, June 24—Personal Time

My mind is vibrating with questions, Journal. I am hoping that if I keep writing, I will get calm again, like how I used to get calm when I first started writing all this stuff down. Except it's not working anymore. Instead it's like the more I dwell on what really happened, the more the questions keep turning and turning round and round inside my brain. I have to figure this out! And now Mrs. Shield is mad at me, I know she is. She might not even want to help me anymore. I think she has given up on me.

Everyone is abandoning me! I even feel abandoned by Nate and Renata, even though I know it's not their fault! What's happening with them? Are they even alive? Why can't I see them? How can I keep doing this without being able to talk to my friends! ! !

Question: What happened between Nate and Chase a long time ago? Why didn't Nate ever tell me what really happened?

Question: What does Chase know about Nate? And what does he know about Renata? What are the big secrets that he is holding over their heads? And why did Renata tell Chase her secret after how much he hurt her in the first place? And WHAT IS HER SECRET?

Question: Why am I still so completely in the dark about all of this? Is there something wrong with me? Am I like the stupid one? Does everyone think I'm a person who can't handle the truth? Not just my mom, but EVERYONE?

How am I ever going to get to the bottom of this? I have to get calm. I have to get calm. I have to get calm. Breathe. Breathe. Breathe. I have to write the rest. I have to write the rest and then maybe I will get some relief.

Breathe. Write the rest. Breathe. Get it over with. *Breathe*. Write it down. Breathe. Do it now.

CD: *Why do I get the feeling that you're avoiding me, Warden Girl?*

Me: *Don't call me that. And I am not avoiding you. I just prefer to pretend you don't exist.*

CD: *Oh, but I do exist, Warden Girl.*

Me: Right, you exist and you're disgusting.

CD: And you're not disgusting? With your spooky lesbo friend and your weirdo boyfriend and your insane mother? Yeah, that's right, you heard me—your insane mother. I know a thing or two about Claire Havenga.

Me: What are you talking about? There's no way you know anything about my mother, you liar.

CD: Oh no? Claire Havenga who works at the Domestic Crisis Center? And who had you when she was a teenager? And who never got married? And so you never met your dad? That Claire Havenga? How am I doing, Warden Girl?

Me: How do you know all that?

CD: My mother told me. She knows everything about everybody in this town, including your mother. It comes in very handy sometimes.

Me: Wait, your mom talked to you about my mom?

CD: Bingo.

Me: So . . . is your mom like . . . friends with my mom?

CD: Oh, I wouldn't call it friendship. It's more like a professional non-friendship. Apparently your momma recently tried to get me into some serious trouble, but it didn't work.

Me: *What kind of serious trouble? Is this about Nate?*

CD: *This has nothing to do with Nate. This has to do with a certain very messed-up girl who told your mother something about me. And because my name was mentioned, your mother called my mother and made the mistake of threatening the great Lenora Dobson. And then my mother said something real loud to your mother. Something that I totally overheard. And then she hung up the phone and told me that your mom would never bother us or anyone related to us ever again. And do you want to know why?*

Me: *No.*

CD: *Oh, I think you do.*

I didn't want to give him the satisfaction of acting interested. Plus I had a feeling that whatever he told me was going to be pretty bad. Like it was going to hurt me. He knows things, Journal. Things he's not supposed to know. He's always hurting people with what he knows about them. So I left the room.

. . .

But I knew I'd have to hear it eventually. And I was right. Sure enough, he told me the next day—Thursday, the day he finally went home.

He also told us that he was going to go with the

kidnapping story. The story where we kidnapped him and forced him to take pills for six days. He said if we didn't go along with the kidnapping story, he'd tell everybody at school what he had found out about us. He'd make sure the whole world knew what he knew. About each one of us. In great detail. He had already told us in private exactly what he was going to reveal. I don't know what Renata's and Nate's secrets were, but mine was about my mom. He told me something really, really bad about my mom, Journal. It was so awful that I went numb all over and couldn't speak for a moment. Couldn't make a single sound come out of my mouth. I thought: it can't be true. But then right away, the very next thought was: it's true.

It's hard to explain. It was just like the something that had been hiding in the shadows behind everything else in my life. All the things my mom could never tell me. And then there it was—the truth.

Chase was waiting for my reaction. I snapped out of it and just tried really hard to act like it was no big deal.

Me: Oh please. How can you possibly think I don't know that already?

CD: I don't know, Warden Girl. Maybe you did already know it. I don't really care. What I'm saying is that if you tell ANYBODY what really happened here, if you tell ANYBODY that I stayed here of my own free will, then EVERYONE will know what I know. Everyone will know what a freak you are.

And it will make your life hell. Worse than it ever was before. So either you can spend a few weeks in juvie for kidnapping me, or you can spend four years of high school in hell. Your choice, Katie.

And somehow I managed to say: Nothing will be worse than being around you. I would take any other kind of hell over that.

But as soon as he went back into the laundry room, I started to cry. I fell down to my knees and put my hands over my mouth and just cried and cried and cried, but softly, so no one would hear. It explained so many things, so many things, Journal. So many things I have been wondering about my whole entire life. My mom would never give me a straight answer.

"He wasn't husband material."

"He wasn't ready to be a father."

"He moved away and never told me where he was going."

"He probably changed his name and so I wouldn't be able to find him."

No wonder she couldn't tell me. How could she even find the words to tell me the real story? How could I even begin to tell her I KNOW the real story? Oh God, it's time for gym. I have to stop. I still haven't written down what he told me. I can't. I'm afraid if I put it into words on paper, I'll die.

Social Worker

Friday, June 25

The social worker was waiting in her car in a small parking lot at the entrance to the Renaissance Medical Arts building in downtown Hamilton, thirty minutes south of North Holmes. It was 8:45 A.M. and already blindingly hot. She'd been waiting since 8:30, with the windows rolled up, listening to the morning news, idling the car, keeping the air conditioning low. The coach had called early and told her that she had a good chance of seeing Chase Dobson in the flesh on Friday morning at the entrance to this building if she got there before 9:00, when the facility opened. He had learned from another coach at the high school that young Chase was being treated for an unknown condition by an unknown physician at this facility.

"None of the coaches have seen Chase since he came home after the incident. But the soccer coach got a letter from the family explaining that Chase wouldn't be available for any morning practices on Fridays all throughout the coming fall semester. The coach called Chase's dad and found out that he sees a doctor of some sort at this medical center in Harrison."

"What sort of a doctor?" Greta asked.

"No idea," the coach admitted. "But you might be able to at least get a good look at him. I would join you, but I'm booked the next few Fridays with private tennis lessons. I want to talk to you about my visit last night too. How about I call you back?"

The social worker was glad he was busy. She preferred to spy without distraction.

At 8:50, from a short distance away, she saw a Mercedes pull slowly into the other side of the parking lot and recognized Lenora Dobson behind the wheel. Greta had parked under a tree, hoping to be safely in shadows; even so, she lowered her head, letting her hair cover the side of her face. Lenora emerged, clutching a white purse. She stood waiting for her passenger to get out, which he did, very slowly. Lenora locked the door and said something to her son as he began a slow stroll away from the car without looking at her. Lenora pitched her keys into her purse, straightened her tight skirt, and followed him.

At the edge of parking lot, she called out something that made him turn around and wait for her. His hair was much longer than the hair on the boy in the video; it curled freely at the sides of his head to his shoulders. He was unusually pale for a North Holmes teenager in the summer, wearing a faded T-shirt and shorts that appeared to have been cut off raggedly from a pair of old corduroys. But the biggest surprise, after seeing him in his carefully recorded athletic glory, was the way he was walking—small steps, hunched shoulders, keeping his arms close; he walked awkwardly, with an air of resignation. He was not carrying himself like an athlete and he appeared slightly overweight. His mother, walking her no-nonsense walk in three-inch heels, caught up with him easily. She put a hand on his hunched shoulder, guiding him closer to the entrance.

Lenora opened the door for Chase and mother and son disappeared into the building.

That was Chase Dobson? Greta asked herself. She sat in her car, considering ways she might see Chase up close without bumping into Lenora, wishing she'd brought a hat with her, something that would have hidden her face more. Instead, she pulled the elastic band out of her hair, fluffed it forward with her fingertips and, on impulse, pulled a relatively dark lipstick from her purse—a shade she seldom wore during the day—slicked it onto her lower lip and exited her car. The disguise was thin, but it was worth the risk for another glimpse of Chase.

Inside the building, she realized instantly that it was unlikely that she would see either Lenora or Chase before they disappeared into whatever office their appointment

233

was in. She did a quick tour of the building, from the first to the third floor, noticing that the facility housed a variety of medical services, everything from dentistry, to chiropractic, to physical therapy, to psychological counseling, many of them behind closed doors in separate suites. No one else was wandering the hallways, as she was doing, perhaps because the building had just opened. She went back to the entrance, found a bench not far from the elevator, and waited.

After forty-five minutes, the elevator opened and Lenore came barreling out without a glance at Greta. Chase came out of the elevator more slowly, walking a good ten feet behind his mother, and so the social worker was able to lift her head from where she sat and take in the sight of him as he came closer. Chase stared back at her, but numbly, without curiosity or surprise. Their eyes met. The social worker was aware of an unwashed smell. There was a sheen of perspiration on his blank face. After he passed, the social worker sat stiffly, noting the fading sound of Lenora's high heels on the floor. The two of them exited through the same doors they had come through earlier.

Once they had exited, the social worker moved again, heading for the door, hurrying for a last glance of them in the parking lot. From inside the building, she watched them walk back to the car, Lenora leading this time. After Chase settled in on the passenger side, they drove away.

. . .

Inside her car, Greta dialed Claire Havenga's number. When Claire didn't answer, she left a message reporting that Katie had specifically written that she was missing her mother. "She might be more willing to talk to you now." As she ended the call, she had a related thought—perhaps Claire's technique would also work for her. Perhaps Katie would also miss her social worker if she kept a distance. She decided to wait a few days before requesting a meeting with Katie. She would instead focus her attention on Nate, on the mystery of his relationship with Chase, and on the deeper, older mystery of why his father had been banished from his family.

· · ·

Nate came into her office carrying a torn sheet from a yellow pad, folded in half. He handed it to her wordlessly before he sat in the chair beside her desk. The page was completely filled, front and back; he never wrote on both sides in his journal. His meticulous handwriting was uncharacteristically scrawled. Nate seemed faintly ashamed. After he handed the single page to her, he put his elbows on his knees and lowered his head into his arms.

"Are you okay?" she asked.

"Read it," he replied.

She put the page on her desk, flattening it with one hand, but before she could begin, he lifted his head and said accusingly, "I had to borrow that crappy paper because you still have my journal. Why didn't you give it back to me? Why didn't you ask to see me?"

"Nate, I've just been really busy."

"Why are you calling me Nate?"

"I'm sorry . . . Nathaniel."

He lowered his head again and she lowered hers to the page—untangling the first paragraph, then the second, then the third, reading quickly, searching for a shred of information beyond what she already knew. She flipped the page over.

"Wait a minute," she said. "You're changing your story about your father? You're saying now that he abandoned you?"

A brief, controlled nod.

"I see. And so do you know the reason he won't come back to North Holmes?"

No response. She kept going. "Did he do something that makes it impossible for him to come back? Did he get into some kind of trouble, Nathaniel?"

"No."

"Nathaniel, you can tell me. Did your father do something hurtful to someone in your family?"

Losing patience. "You don't understand. My dad would never hurt anyone. He was noble. God. I don't want to talk about this anymore."

"Okay." She finished the page and folded it in half. "Thank you for bringing me this."

"You're welcome. I've been really worried. I thought you were giving up on me."

"I would never give up on you! Even though you refuse to tell me what happened, I'm figuring it out, Nathaniel. I'm going to figure out what happened whether any of you tell me or not. But the whole thing is making me too busy to meet with you as often as I would like to."

"I just . . . I had a couple of really bad days, Mrs. Shield," he said. "My sister tried to visit me again."

"When?"

"Yesterday. Right after I wrote that one page. I didn't go to the Visitor's Room, I didn't want to talk to her. I was in no shape to see her. I told Carl to tell her I was sick. Which I sort of was. I feel really hopeless the last few days. About what's going to happen to me."

"I don't want you to feel hopeless. I've actually had some good days. I'm making real progress. I especially wanted to tell you that I saw Chase Dobson this morning."

Nate was surprised. "How could you see him? Did you . . . go to his house?"

"No. Somewhere else. I didn't actually speak with him, but I saw his face. And I wanted to tell you that he looked terrible. Not like a champion at all. More like someone recovering from a terrible illness. And I wondered if there is anything you can tell me about why he would be looking so ill three weeks after you and the girls released him."

"Was he alone?" Nate asked, almost whispering.

"No, he was with his mother."

Nate shook his head, as though this wasn't possible. "He hates his mother, Mrs. Shield. He makes sure to never be alone with either one of his parents."

"Well, he was with his mother this morning. She was walking him into a medical center. Can you tell me why he might need a doctor?"

When Nate didn't answer, she pressed, "Would it have something to do with the drugs you and the girls gave him?"

Nate grimaced. The social worker had the impression that he was struggling not to overreact, perhaps sorting through facts in his mind, deciding what he could safely tell her. Finally, he waved his hands and blurted pleadingly, "Okay, okay, okay! Ask me if Chase took too many pills."

A pause. "Did Chase take too many pills?"

"Way too many! Especially at the end. I warned him!"

"That's not what the police report says. The police report said you and the others administered drugs to him *against his will*. It's one of several reasons that you are in such serious trouble. Are you listening to me? You could spend a long time in here. If you did not actually force Chase to take the drugs, you really need to tell me."

"The drug stuff is a big part of the pact, Mrs. Shield!"

"Can you write about it?"

"No! I can't write about it either!"

"Can you make it fiction? Change the names of the characters?"

He shook his head solemnly. "I've already told you too much. You would totally know that it's about Chase."

A standoff. The social worker hid her disappointment and excused him, arranged for him to be escorted back to his classroom.

. . .

The phone rang and when the social worker picked up, Natalie Wilson said in a hushed voice, "Could you please hang up, Mrs. Shield? I was about to leave you a message."

"Excuse me?"

"I'm not allowed to talk to you, but if I just leave a message, that won't be talking to you, right? Okay? Ooops, I'm talking to you." She hung up before the social worker could respond.

The phone rang again a moment later. Voice mail picked up the message—Natalie in a breathless voice: "Okay, I found my dad's phone number in Cleveland. At least, I'm pretty sure it's my dad's number, I found it in a drawer—it's just a number. No name or address. My mom would kill me if she knew I was doing this. When you talk to my dad, could you tell me what he says? Oh, wait, I'm not supposed to talk to you. Could you leave me a message? But don't tell Nate. I tried to see him. I'm praying for him every day. Okay, here's the number."

 Nathaniel, Son of James

Evening: Don't you understand, Great She? The Master had bound me with invisible chains. The Master owns me still. The Master will tell the world about the Great Disappearance. And if he does that, all is lost for me. My fate is in the Master's hands. As his is in mine. Yet I would never betray him, for I am Nathaniel, Chief Grey-Mount, Son of James. He has promised not to betray me, and I believe that he will keep that promise, but only to protect the greater secret of his own dark heart. And I know that he is more of a prisoner in his room full of trophies than I am here in my empty cell. He is more of an exile in his mind than I am behind prison walls. I know his story, I know his crime. A story of Destruction! Calamity! Deception!

But my story is sadder, Great She. His story is terrible, but my story is pure bitter sadness. And the Master knows. The Master has seen me in my wretchedness as I have seen him in his. This is why he has exacted such a terrible price of me and my sisters.

I am telling you that he still has power over me, Great She. He may be sick, and he may be seeing a doctor, but he rules me and silences me still.

You say he looked "terrible." You ask me to explain his demise, he who once commanded the great halls and the open fields of the arena, he who had legions serving and protecting him. You said he appeared to be in servitude to his mother, whom I know he despises, as I despise my own mother for her weakness and her delusions, for we also spoke of this, Great She. We spoke of this in our brief confessions, those long-past disclosures that I have paid so dearly for. The Master's mother is not weak, nor blind, nor at the mercy of the one she calls husband; in fact, she is more powerful than her husband, as she was more powerful than the father of her husband while he lived, the first champion who was found at the bottom of the sea. If the Master is in the clutches of his mother, then he is in his hell, as I am in mine. She will force him to return to the path of the champion and he will not be able to deny her. She will make him strong again, yet he will become even more like her. It saddens me, Great She, even though the Master is dead to me now. At one time, very briefly, I believed that he might change and that our friendship, forged in loss, would survive. Because of what we knew about each other and because we had both once lived in the company of champions. Kings. Patriarchs. But no more.

The Master will destroy me if I do not keep my promises and he will destroy my sisters if they do not also keep their promises. I have no doubt of that now, although it was not always so. It was not always so. There was a brief time of forgiveness and hope. But it is no more. Not if the Master is in servitude to his mother.

And as for my blood sister, she who comes to me unbidden with her false humility and her allegiance to the Queen of Shadows—when they told me she had come to see me, my despair was so great that I feared the mere sight of her would plunge me into the abyss. And so I would not see her, and it was a great relief to know that she was gone, hopefully never to return, for she cannot help me and can only remind me of the emptiness I face when I leave the Place of Contrition.

I do long to leave, Great She, for I long to be free and to see my true sisters and to walk along the shores of the sea where I once swam with my father. But nothing will be the same for me once I leave here, and there is no possible way that I can reside under the same roof as the Queen of Shadows. Nor can I live in the place called Cleves— a place where I did not see my father, but rather fell for many days into a pit of chaos. It took all the strength I had to find my way back home, only to realize that my home was not my home. There is no home for me. There is no place in the world right now where I am safe.

The closest I thing I ever felt to a home was being in my first GreyMount's kitchen with her mother making soup, or being in my second GreyMount's blue bedroom, lying on the great bed with both my sisters, sharing ideas for my next story. Now both my sisters sleep on barren cots surrounded by stone walls. They dress in rags and turn to face the wall when I walk by. And they are both innocent. Especially Katie, my first GreyMount, she of the purest, kindest heart, she who walks with her head high and is never distracted by fools in her unwavering nobility. She who faced the wall in disgrace like a punished schoolgirl, all because of me.

I am lost, Great She. I don't know how much longer I can last in here. I wish I could tell you everything, but there is danger all around me and it will be worse when I get out if I do not keep my promises.

Social Worker

Saturday, June 26

If James Wilson truly did not yet know that Nate was in detention, there would be much to explain to him very quickly. As she dialed, her concern for Nate rose to the surface of her skin—her throat was dry, her hands damp, the scalp under her elastic headband itchy. She listened as the phone rang once, twice, three times—all the while rehearsing a quick explanation for the complicated nature of her call. *Your son has been in juvenile detention for several weeks, Mr. Wilson. I am his social worker. I'm afraid he is in very serious trouble. . . .*

A woman answered on the fourth ring. The social worker took a deep breath and spoke in her most somber and professional voice. "This is Greta Shield from the

Ferndale Juvenile Court System in North Holmes, Michigan. Is Mr. James Wilson available?"

"James Wilson?" the woman repeated.

"Yes, is there a James Wilson at this number?"

A long pause. The voice dropped almost to a whisper. "Who did you say you were with?"

"My name is Greta Shield. I'm a social worker in North Holmes. I work with juveniles in detention. I have something very important to discuss with James Wilson if he is available."

Another long pause. "Is this about Nate?" the woman asked.

"I'm afraid it is. May I speak with Mr. Wilson please?"

"My name is Janine," the woman said. "I used to be James Wilson. Please tell me what has happened to my son."

. . .

"We talked for almost an hour."

The social worker and Claire Havenga were walking along a bike path near the Domestic Crisis Center, where Clair had also been working on a Saturday. The social worker was trying to reconstruct her conversation with Janine Wilson.

"He—I mean she—didn't know anything about Nate being in detention. Nothing. Sylvia Wilson hadn't told him . . . her. Janine is not allowed to have any contact with the children. Sylvia got a court order after he decided to go through with becoming a woman and James . . . Janine has never challenged it."

"That's not unusual," Claire said. "I've seen it happen. The courts can prohibit visitation and they often do. Many transgendered parents are forced to leave their children behind. It's a terrible price to pay, but amazingly, people pay it. For some, it's the difference between living and dying."

"Did Katie ever mention that Nate took a trip to Cleveland to see his father?"

"Oh God," Claire said. "Is that how he found out?"

"I think so. It was last winter—Katie never mentioned it to you?"

"I doubt if she knows. She always said that Nate had a fully functioning dad with a job in Cleveland. Poor Nate, carrying this burden all alone."

"When I questioned him about it a week ago, he looked me in the eye and said he went to Cleveland but didn't see his father. It wasn't a lie, Claire.

"No . . . he didn't see his father."

"Instead he met . . . Janine. She said the encounter was an absolute disaster."

"Katie doesn't know," Claire decided.

"Janine said she tried writing to him afterward, but her letters were sent back unread, and she was never sure if it was Nate sending them back or Sylvia."

"This is just too sad, Greta."

"So I have a new theory," Greta announced. "I think

Nate told Chase about his father last summer. Told Chase that his father had become a woman. I think Chase is the only person he's ever told."

"Of all the people to tell—I can't believe it would be that horrible boy!"

"It was a moment, Claire. Nate thought they might become friends. And I think Nate told him his deepest darkest secret in exchange for something Chase told him. Nate mentioned this very early on in his journal. Something that the two told each other in a highly emotional state. And at the time Nate saw it as a bond of friendship. And something to fill the void left by his father's disappearance. But then Chase began to punish Nate for what he knew."

"Bullies can't stand to have anyone know they are suffering."

"Chase went after Renata to punish Nate. He might have even thought that she was his girlfriend. Since they were always together."

"It's very possible."

"But here's something I still haven't figured out—what did Chase tell Nate? What kind of a secret would compare in importance to Nate's secret?"

"That boy has plenty of secrets. Lots of stuff that would have gotten him into serious trouble if he hadn't been a Dobson."

"I know. But I don't know what he told Nate that night."

"Nate won't tell you?"

"Apparently he and Chase made a pact. It's almost . . . religious, this thing he has about not breaking a promise. He's just . . . he's just so . . . honorable."

As they turned back toward the DCC, Claire spoke again. "I've been thinking about Renata. About some things I said when I first met you. Remember I said I didn't trust her?"

"You said she was deliberately secretive."

"She kept her distance from me. And so I assumed she wasn't good for Katie. But, really, I was jealous. Katie adored her. Like instantly. Unconditionally, as soon as they met. And Katie didn't want to share her new friend with me. I resented that so much. So when I learned how much trouble Katie was in, I blamed Renata. I'm ashamed of that now. Teen advocate . . . heal thyself."

• • •

Back in the social worker's office, she noticed that Martin had left a voice mail. She dialed his cell phone number, curious about how his second visit with Renata had gone.

"When I got to the JDC, I was told she already had visitors. So I went back to the parking lot for a little while, watching other visitors come and go. I noticed one odd couple. And older man and an attractive woman with a cane."

"That was her parents. Interesting. What did her father look like?"

"Well, like I said, much older than his wife. Grey hair in a ponytail. Both of them looked pretty artsy, almost like foreigners, dressed in black in the middle of summer. But even from a distance, I could tell that they were both upset. Looked like the mother might have been crying."

"Amazing," the social worker exclaimed softly.

"The woman was walking with a bad limp. What's wrong with her?"

"A car accident. Before she came to North Holmes."

"What a shame. Anyway, I'm sorry I wasn't able to complete my assignment. What about you? Did you call Nate Wilson's father?"

The social worker hesitated. "I'll tell you about it another time," she said. "Right now, I'm very busy."

"Are you at your office?"

"No," Greta lied. "It's Saturday."

She stayed in her office, attending to other tasks for a few more hours. As she was straightening her desk to leave, she decided it was time to check in with Katie. Ten minutes later, Katie was escorted into her office. Like Nate, she was carrying a single sheet of paper, but unlike Nate, she didn't hand it over to the social worker immediately; instead she held it, folded into quarters, in one hand, flapping it against her thigh as though she wasn't sure she was ready to part with it.

The social worker pointed to it. "Did you finally write something helpful?"

"I wrote something about Chase. You can read it if you want to."

"Hand it over." The social worker flattened the page on her desk and scanned it. The final paragraph gave her pause: *the secret that Chase Dobson knows about me would just like really, really destroy my mom if people knew.* Greta lifted her head and gazed at Katie, who was holding one fist tightly against her mouth.

"That's all I can say, Mrs. Shield."

The social worker refolded the paper slowly. "Did you see your mother earlier this afternoon?" she asked.

"She came. I told her you were mad at me, but she said you're not."

"I'm not mad at any of you. But let's be clear. Are you saying that Chase Dobson knows something about you that could hurt your mother very much?"

She nodded again, suddenly fighting tears.

"And you know . . . what it is that Chase knows?"

"Yes, but I don't want Mom to know that I know."

"Are you afraid she wouldn't be able to handle it?"

Another nod. "She's been through a lot, Mrs. Shield."

"And how do you think Chase came to know what your mom . . . has been though?"

Katie closed her eyes, thinking. "Well . . . Chase has a mother who knows things. About people in this town. I guess she even knew my mom. Not like as a friend, but . . . well . . . anyway, her name is Lenora Dobson. Have you ever heard of her?"

"Oh, I have," the social worker reported mildly. She leaned closer to where Katie was sitting. "Do you by any chance know the secret thing that Nate knows about Chase?"

"No," Katie said without hesitation. "Nate wouldn't tell us. Because he promised never to tell. Plus he said it was better if I didn't know."

"Does Renata know more than you? With her gift of knowing-without-being-told?"

This startled Katie. "How do you know about that?"

"Nate mentioned it in his journal. Apparently he didn't think writing about that was breaking the pact."

Katie's eyes got rounder. "You know about the pact too?"

"I sensed it from the beginning."

"Do you believe in Renata's gift, Mrs. Shield? My mom didn't believe it. I tried to tell her about it once and she laughed at me. She never listened to anything I said about Renata."

"She might be more ready to listen now."

"Why do you think that?"

"I think your mom is . . . rethinking some things."

"I am too, Mrs. Shield! I'm seriously rethinking things. But I'm so confused about what I can tell you and what I can't tell you. We made the pact in a rush at the end and then before we knew it, we were in here and we couldn't talk to each other about anything anymore."

"I understand."

Katie sighed. "It seems like you do understand. And you don't seem as worried about me anymore."

"Oh, I'm still worried," the social worker said.

Monday, June 28

Nate Wilson was rocking to and fro in the chair beside the social worker's desk, weeping into his long-fingered hands. "She drove him to it! She drove him to it, Mrs. Shield!"

"Nathaniel, you can't blame your mother for his decision."

The boy uncovered his glistening face. "But I do, Mrs. Shield. I do. She's a complete psycho! Nobody could live with her! Nobody could stand to be married to her!"

"Your father could have just filed for divorce. What he did is something very, very different."

Nate covered his face again and spoke through his fingers. "Why couldn't he have just died?"

"Nathaniel."

"Like in some really mysterious, tragic way, you know? Then I could have helped my little brothers get over it. I would have known what to say. I could have been strong for them. But what am I supposed to say about this? How am I supposed to help them? I can't even think about it. I have to work so hard not to think about it." Emotions strangled his voice. I was his favorite, Mrs. Shield. I know I was. I know I was."

Now he had a hand, clawlike, on each knee, but he

was still rocking, his face contorted. It was almost more than the social worker could bear. She looked at the clock, alarmed to see that their time was almost up. "We are going to talk more about this—you and I—but right now I have to ask you something else—something really important. Because we don't have much time left this morning. I'm going to speak with your lawyer this afternoon about some of the things I've learned this week, but first I need you to listen carefully to one more important question. So I want you to focus. Please, Nathaniel. Focus with me."

"Okay, okay, okay." He took a deep shuddering breath.

"Is there anyone besides you and me and your mother who knows that your father changed his gender?"

The social worker watched a series of emotions play across Nate's face. She put a hand over each of his hands, where they were still clasped on his knees, taking a chance that touching him this way would bring him back to the act of confiding in her. "Who else knows?"

No answer, more rocking.

"Does Katie know?"

He shook his head fiercely, no.

"Does Renata know?"

"No." Another fierce shake.

"So no one knows about James of Cleves except your mother?"

Nate groaned at the mention of his mother.

"And is this the secret you told Chase in the little room?"

He uncovered his face and exclaimed softly, "I never told you!"

"No, you didn't tell me. You didn't have to tell me. But then there was the other promise, right? The pact you made with the girls before you came here? You all made a promise not to tell what really happened at Renata's house, didn't you?"

Nodded. "It was so that he wouldn't tell what he knew about . . . us."

"And who was he going to tell?"

"The whole world, Mrs. Shield."

"Right," she said. "The whole world. Of course. Of course."

. . .

Renata sat straight-backed in the social worker's stuffed chair, a very different pose, a very different girl from the one who had curled up in misery against the cushions just three weeks ago, weeping profusely. She seemed calm on this Monday morning, almost cheerful. She seemed to have come into her own in the past week and the social worker wondered why. "Is there something you want to tell me, Renata?"

Renata smiled mysteriously. "They have forgiven me. Even my mother. They came twice to see me. And she promised to help me. She said that as soon as I was free, we would start over. She shed tears for me. I have never seen her cry like that before, not even when . . ." She caught herself and pressed her lips together.

"Not even when . . . ?"

Renata said carefully, "Not even when we had problems in the past."

"Problems?"

"A long time ago. Before I came here."

"Does it have something to do with your mother's injuries?" the social worker asked.

Renata paled. She said, a brisk formality coming back into her voice, "It is not relevant to the case."

"Are you sure?"

Renata cleared her throat. "I am not free to discuss it," she said. "Anyway, Mrs. Shield, I was wondering how my friends are doing. I am very concerned about them."

The social worker counterattacked. "Things would be better for your friends if you would tell me what Chase Dobson's secret is. I have a feeling you know."

Renata's mouth fell open.

Greta zeroed in. "That's right. Chase's secret is from before the pact. So you are not breaking the pact if you talk to me about it." She paused for emphasis. "Do you follow me?"

"Yes," Renata agreed softly.

"I happen to know that you are very good at reading people, Renata; Nate told me about your gift."

"And do you believe in my gift, Mrs. Shield?" She asked this as though the social worker's answer would hold the key.

"Yes, I do."

Renata closed her eyes, taking this in. She put her hands in her lap, one atop the other, and she tipped her head back, savoring the fact that the social worker believed in her gift.

Then she reported softly, "Sometimes what I see in my mind is very chaotic. I have to focus and listen very carefully. Which can be hard, if you're at school or in a place like this. It's why I like to stay in my room. And why I need to draw. The images and the voices help me find the answers."

Greta listened patiently, inwardly dying to get back to the subject of Chase.

Perhaps Renata sensed this. She took a deep, steadying breath. "Way back when Chase first started attacking me, I knew there was something wrong with him. Something he had done. Something people didn't know. And on the last night at my house, he told me what he did. And then . . . and then I told him something that I did. Something I should never have told him. Katie warned me not to trust him."

She waved her hands at the sides of her face, as though to erase the memory of her mistake.

"Renata," the social worker pleaded softly. "For the sake of your friends who may not come out of this as well as you will, please, please, tell me what you know about Chase. Just this one little thing."

"Oh, it's not little, Mrs. Shield," Renata whispered. "It's huge."

"Can you make me a drawing about it?" The social worker rang for security. "Go back to your pod now and make me a new drawing. Bring it to me as soon as it's done."

At the doorway, Renata announced softly, "People think I'm weak because I'm small. My whole life people have thought that. But I'm not weak. I wasn't going to be the one who broke the pact."

"Right. Got it. You didn't break the pact. Now go make me that drawing."

Alone, she opened the file on her desk of Renata's earlier drawings and studied them. Then she impulsively dialed Lenora Dobson's cell phone number and left a message:

"Lenora, this is Greta Shield from the Ferndale JDC. Sorry to bother you , but I need to talk to you as soon as possible about some concerns I have regarding the boating accident last July that resulted in your father-in-law's tragic death. I'm sorry to have to bring up this painful subject, but a few things have come up in my work with the juveniles who allegedly abducted your son, one of whom did in fact know your son long before his disappearance in May. I need some clarification about the boating accident, and I'm hoping that you can provide it. Please call me as soon as you are able."

The truth of the case was close to the surface—she was sure of it. She could almost make it out. Still, she had a huge afternoon ahead of her—catching up with her other caseloads and checking in with half a dozen new residents. She had two preliminary meetings to fit into the next twenty-four hours. It was time for her to wrench her attention away from the keepers of the pact.

Tuesday, June 28

The next day Greta was compiling notes from preliminary meetings, when the facility's assistant supervisor rapped on her slightly ajar door and poked his head inside. Greta hid the fact that she was unsettled to see him; Frank Messinger came directly to her office only when something was amiss. "Frank, come in," she said. "What can I help you with?"

"Just got word from the court, Greta. Bit of a shocker, but thought you should hear it early. The prosecuting attorney just dropped all the charges against your young kidnappers. Nobody seems to know why. Any ideas?"

Greta was astounded. "The attorney did *what*?"

"Dropped the charges. All of them. Completely. End of story. I'm assuming the Dobson family requested it. Did you have any sense that this was coming?"

"No, of course not. I can't believe it! Have my kids been notified? Should I call them in here right now?"

"No, the Shift Supervisor will tell them. You just let him handle it, Greta. They'll all be sent home as soon as we get ahold of the parents."

"Oh, let me do that, Frank. I still have some questions. . . ."

"I'm sorry to put it this way, Greta, but there is a sense among the other staff that you've gone way overboard in your involvement with this case. Let it go. You need to catch up with your other residents."

Greta could not argue with him. She knew that it was true—she had let the case take over her workday and her weekends and her imagination. But to turn away now... when she was so close to knowing the truth. She thought of her call to Lenora, replaying it in her mind. What had caused her to request that the prosecuting attorney drop the charges? She said softly, "I wasn't threatening her. I just wanted to talk to her."

"Talk to who?" Frank asked. "What are you referring to?"

"Nothing," she insisted. "I'll get back to work now on my new cases. Thank you for the update, Frank."

She was dismissing him, wanting him to leave. She needed to be alone. She needed to understand what had just happened. She decided to go over everything she had on the Dobson case one last time. She would need privacy. She got up from her desk and was about to lock her door when Shift Supervisor Dan appeared in the hallway, waving a sheet of paper in her direction.

"Brought you something," he called. "Renata said you assigned her this drawing yesterday."

"Yes, I did," Greta said. "Thank you very much."

She took it out of his hands and shut her door quickly, locking it. Renata had been right. Chase's secret was huge.

Renata's Journal

First GreyMount Katie

Woohoo! Lee Ann told me that all the charges against us were dropped I can go home as soon as they get ahold of my mom to come and pick me up which might take a little while because she's working today, but I don't care. I can wait. I'm so happy and the really great thing is that we don't have to go back to court! I don't know how this happened, but WE KEPT OUR PROMISE AND WE DIDN'T BREAK THE PACT!

So I already cleaned my room, and I changed into my clothes, and I have some time to fill before my mom comes and I am wondering: do I need to tell the rest of it, Journal? Do I need to fill up another page with words that nobody but me will ever see? I want to. Something makes me think that if I keep writing, it will help me. It will help me to move on and look to the future. Maybe it will even help me to figure out the stuff I haven't quite figured out yet. Then I will be even braver. Brave as Nate. Brave as Renata. Brave as Mom.

I will write it and then I will throw it into the trash bag Lee Ann gave me and no one will ever, ever see it. But I must write it anyway. Because I am a GreyMount. And because I am innocent. And because I didn't break the pact. And because I am going home.

It was after school on Friday, the last day. Chase was taking his nap and we were in Renata's kitchen. I put my hand on Nate's hand, to get his attention, something I never did because Nate doesn't like to be touched unless it's absolutely necessary.

Me: Nate. Nate, listen. There is something about me that nobody knows.

Nate: There is something about me that nobody knows too.

Me: Really?

Nate: Really.

Me: Is your thing bad?

Nate: Yeah.

Me: Mine too.

Nate: Is your thing about your dad?

Me: How did you know?

Nate: I didn't. It's just that . . . my thing is about my dad.

Me: Really?

Nate: Really.

Me: I think my thing might be worse than your thing.

Nate: I doubt it.

We heard Chase groaning from his room. I think he might have been having a nightmare. The sound was terrible—a long groan ending in a kind of scream.

Me: Chase knows the secret about my dad, Nate.

Nate: Oh my God. You told him?

Me: I didn't tell him. I would never tell him anything. I try not to talk to him at all. I try not to even LOOK at him. But he's tricky. He found out . . . some other way.

Nate: You don't have to tell me what your secret about your dad is. Because I can't even begin to tell you what mine is.

Me: Chase told me that he would tell the world my secret if I didn't go along with his story. The one he's going to tell his parents when he goes home about us making him take drugs. Did he say the same thing to you?

Nate: Yes.

Me: Oh God. Does Renata have a secret too?

Nate: Yes.

Me: Do you know what it is?

Nate: No. It's just . . . I have a feeling it's something that happened before she came here. Before we met her.

Me: Do you think Chase knows Renata's secret?

Nate: He has this way of making people tell him things, Katie. It's how he controls people. He's like a master of controlling people.

Me: Including you, right?

Nate: It was different with me. We were friends. We were. For a very short time, but it was real. I saw him the way he really is. I saw his pain.

Me: [Losing my temper] He's going to blackmail us! All three of us! That's the kind of friend he is. He's just . . . EVIL. I said it from day one but you just refused to listen to me. Because you think you're so much smarter than me. But I was right. I was right all along. I didn't want to do this. Why didn't either of you listen to me? Why didn't you let me protect you?

Then we were both crying. In the next room, Chase was groaning even louder, calling something, someone's name, I couldn't figure out who it was. Nate heard it too and he covered his face, like it was killing him to hear it.

We were still crying when Renata came in from the little party store near her house. She had a bag of snacks for Chase—chips and cookies and more cereal. She put the grocery bag down and came over to us and took each of our hands.

We didn't know yet that Chase was going to leave that night. First he would eat all the food Renata brought for him, and then he would threaten us one more time, and then he would leave Renata's house on foot and walk to his mansion on North Shore. He would tell his parents that we had kidnapped him and kept him a prisoner and forced him to take drugs, all because we were jealous of him and because we are three really dangerous loser juvenile delinquents who should be locked up right away before one of them comes to school with a gun.

And then we would be locked up. And we wouldn't even be able to see each other, or talk to each other, not once for days and days and days. We would have been crying a lot harder if we knew that.

nathaniel, Son of Nobody

Journal
Day 23 of Captivity

That's right, Great She. I am Son of Nobody now.

I am still firstborn, still swordsman of my Clan, still scribe and messenger, but I am Son of Nobody. One hour ago I learned that I will be released from the Place of Contrition, but once freed I will remain in a state of exile, with no men in the constellation of my life, no father, no elder brother, no male friends. I have only my true sisters and my writing hand and the knowledge that I was strong enough to keep the pact. I gather these truths around me as I prepare to depart. I am told that I must clean the room I was imprisoned in. Then I will be allowed to change into my own clothes, never to wear my prison rags again. I am told my mother has agreed to come for me. I feel neither joy nor relief at this prospect.

At first I felt relief. When the Prison Steward told me at morning provisions that my release was imminent, I became dizzy with relief. I could not eat. I could not speak. I had to take many deep breaths to control the emotions that surfaced at my reprieve. But as soon as I was alone, cleaning my cell, my relief fell away from me like a veil, revealing the dark shapes of unanswered questions. Why? Why have I been freed? Why is there to be no trial? What has happened? Did one of my sisters break the pact?

Did one of my sisters break the pact, Great She?

But even as I ask you this, I know the answer. My sisters did not break the pact. That is not possible. Something else has secured our release—but what? Is this your doing, Great She? And why have you been "reassigned," as my Prison Steward told me when I asked him if I could see you forthwith? Does it have something to do with my terrible secret? Our last conversation? Have the powers that be in the Place of Contrition decided that you can no longer help me?

I have entreated my Prison Steward to bring you this final journal entry once I have written it. I have some things I must tell you.

Since my last conversation with you, my sister who is not my true sister sent me a letter by mail, written in her clumsy but forceful hand. I received it yesterday. It contained two items that disturbed my sleep last night. The first item involves the Queen of Shadows. Apparently, she has been in close and constant communication with the Pastor at her church, the Chief Collector of Souls in the largest church in North Holmes. I have never liked this Pastor, Great She, he looks at me with jaundiced eye and reproving frown and I never felt the slightest solace or reassurance in his company. The Queen knows this well, but nevertheless she has arranged for me, as a requirement for reentry into the house of my birth, long and intensive counseling from this Pastor as soon as I am released into her custody.

When first I read my birth sister's letter, this news seemed like a distant unpleasantness, something for me to face in the future, but now I am aware that it is at hand, more inescapable and perhaps more excruciating than anything I experienced in my Time of Forced Confession. I wish I could bring my unhappiness at this thought to your doorstep and deliver it to the safety of your generous counsel. But let me just say, Great She, that I will not agree to counseling with the Pastor. I will not. I swear this on my name and on the name of my once-father. I do not know what this will mean for me. Will I be thrown to the streets, homeless and unwanted?

An idea has come to me, Great She, one that I also wish I could share with you face-to-face, sitting in the blue chair of your office, where I so often found solace in my darkest days. I think I am going to ask my First GreyMount if her mother, the Lady of Forgotten Girls, would allow me to live at their house for just a little while upon my release. Until I decide my future path. Have you met my first GreyMount's mother? Have you spoken with her? She has always been kind to me. It is my belief that she cares about me and sees me as I truly am and probably never believed that I was a criminal, capable of the deeds of which I was accused.

The Lady has a little room at the back of their house with a futon and a small desk and an empty bookshelf—it is in fact a sun porch with a painted cement floor, dark red, the color of vitality and strength. I slept there once under woolen blankets during a snowstorm in which it was impossible for me to be driven safely home. I liked waking up in that little room, surrounded by windows. I picture myself in that room again; the light calls out to me—this is an enclosure where I could sort out all of the events of the recent past and plot a path for myself for the coming year. For I will soon walk through peaks and valleys of a new Great Hall. In preparation, I must strengthen my resolve, for I sense more challenges await me, and perhaps more danger.

Which brings me to the second detail of my sister's letter. She says, in her own words, "that kid I kidnapped" has been calling my house, asking her when I will be released. And so from this I know that the Master plans a further reckoning with me, to what end I do not know. I will need strength and focus in the early days of my freedom. Perhaps the Master thinks that I or one of my true sisters broke the pact. Perhaps now he will indeed tell the world what he knows about each of us, as he threatened to do in the days before our arrest and imprisonment. Perhaps the grave secret of my once-father will be brought into the light against all hope.

Perhaps he never intended to keep the pact himself.

I must face what is coming without blame or fear, Great She.

Fear has crippled and hardened and sickened the Master and I do not wish to follow him, nor face him in battle, not seek his friendship. Never again.

In truth the Master barely spoke to me in the final hours of his time of hiding. He was, by then, unsteady of bearing and thick-tongued from the potions of his undoing. At the end, he spoke only to Renata. He could not even meet my eyes until the final moment before he lurched away from us and headed north to his own people. Then he stopped in the circular driveway of the House of Glass and Magic and turned around slowly and stared hard at me, as though remembering who I was, after a long amnesia.

He said my name once. His voice was a ragged croak. And I saw how much he feared me, Great She. His eyes were full of fear. Fear of what I knew and fear of what lay ahead, not for the three of us, but for himself and for his own terrible secret, which I am beginning to realize was worse than my secret. For his secret was a deed committed by his own hand. A great, crashing shipwreck of a deed that can never be undone. While my secret was about something someone else had done. Someone beloved, someone who had left me, as surely as if he had died. Yet I committed no crime, Great She.

Verily, I have made a decision in the final hours of my imprisonment in this place. I wanted you to know of it. Without delay I shall reveal to my two brave GreyMounts the truth about my once-father. I am going to present to them the tragedy of my lost parentage. For isn't it true that they are my sisters and they have walked through fire for me in the Place of Contrition? Have they not proven their faithfulness?

It is my fervent hope that my sisters will accept me, as you yourself accepted me, once you knew my terrible secret.

Please know that I hold you in the highest esteem for your counsel and your kind manner and careful phrases, even though I was not able to tell you directly all of the things that you had hoped I would tell you. Perhaps if you see the Lady who calls herself Claire in the coming days, you could mention to her my idea about staying in the little room at the back of her house and tell her that you think it is a good idea. Perhaps that would make it more likely that she will say yes.

Good-bye, Great She. I am Nathaniel and I am Son of Nobody, but I did not break the pact.

From Katie Havenga to the Visitor's Room Attendant

Please, please, please give these pages to Mrs. Shield!

Hi, Mrs. Shield, Lee Ann told me I couldn't see you face-to-face before I leave. That feels very strange, I figured we would at least get to say good-bye. Right now I am in the Visitor's Room and my mom is on her way over here, but she told the Youth Specialist that she might be a little late because one of her girls at the crisis center is having a nervous breakdown. Like I care, Mom! Get over here! I need to go home! I need to be in my own room and my own bed. And take a real shower.

I don't know where Nate is, but Renata's parents came and took her away already. She was wearing regular clothes (I am too!) and she looked amazing, even though she lost weight in here and her hair is all different crazy lengths. We hugged each other really, really hard when we first saw each other, but we stayed calm. We didn't cry. I told her I was writing something for you and she said she wrote something for you too. She asked me to put it with my pages before I leave. It was a folded up note and a drawing that wasn't folded. I saw that it was a drawing of a car accident, but I didn't want to stare at it in case Renata didn't want me to see it.

Her parents were in a big rush to get her out of here. They didn't want to talk to me, but that's nothing new and it's okay, I don't care. Her dad calls me Kathy—he has never even learned my name. He and Magdalena are probably hoping that Renata won't want to be friends with me anymore, but what do they know? We are sisters. More than ever. After they signed her release, Renata whispered: "Call me tonight!" Then she was gone!

Oh, my God I can do that! I can call her tonight. I can call Nate too. I was even thinking of inviting him to come over to my house on his bike and maybe sleep over if he wants to. I'm going to tell him he can stay in our little porch room if things are too weird back at his own house. The last time my mom visited me, she said that Nate would need a lot of support once he gets out of here. So she was thinking about him too.

There's something I need to do when I get out of here. I wasn't strong enough to do it before, but I think I'm strong enough to do it now. It's because of Chase. I don't want to be afraid of him ever again. So I have to tell my friends the thing that Chase found out about me. I don't want it to be a secret that only he knows. I just have to figure out how to say it. The right words. It will be very hard to explain. But I feel pretty sure that my friends won't reject me once they know. Some people might reject me, but not Nate and not Renata. And I am going to ask them to tell me their secrets too. I hope they will. We have to help each other get through the next year. It could be really bad. We need to stay united!

There's one more thing I have to do and it will be even harder. Like so hard I don't think I can do it right away. But I will do it! I have to tell my mom that I know something that she didn't want me ever to know. Something about how I was born. I think she has been hoping that I would never find out. But that was very unrealistic of her, Mrs. Shield. People say things. People tell things. My mom is so strong, but sometimes she is unrealistic.

Oh my God, I hear my mom's voice in the hall outside the visiting room. She is talking to someone on the staff, someone she probably knew from before I got put in here. She knows a lot of people in this town.

I just looked closer at Renata's drawing. I couldn't stop myself. So now I know that what she drew is her secret. She must have wanted you to know it. Is my secret worse? Hers is very bad. It must have been so awful for her to draw it. I'm going to call her as soon as I get home and tell her that she is still my friend and then I will share my secret with her. I wish I could draw my secret too, so that I wouldn't have to say it. But I will say it. Good-bye, Mrs. Shield.

For Mrs. Shield from Renata

After I drew Chase's secret, I decided to draw my own. Because I don't want it to be a secret anymore. I am so tired of nobody knowing what happened in Charlotte, not even my friends. So I drew this while Dan thought I was cleaning out my room. It tells the truth. My mom is trying to forgive me for what happened in Charlotte, but I don't think I will ever forgive myself.

I want to say one more thing, just to you, Mrs. Shield. Because you listened to me and you believed in my gift and you gave me the sketchbook when I needed it. I wanted to say that even if you didn't figure everything out, like you wanted to, you did do something that helped us. You made us think hard about all of the things we couldn't tell you. Our secrets. And now that we are going to be set free from detention, I think we will also leave the prison of our secrets. We can let the darkness go, like the crows, into the sky over North Holmes. I believe this in my heart, Mrs. Shield. So that is one very good thing that has happened because of you.

Renata

acknowledgments

Several people helped me to make the Ferndale Juvenile Detention Center a realistic setting. First and foremost, I would like to thank Sandi Metcalf, Director of Juvenile Services for the 20th Judicial Circuit Court, who was always encouraging and incredibly generous with her time. I would also like to thank Lily Marx, Detention Superintendent at the JDC in Ottawa County, Michigan, for several tours of the facility and for generously sharing her expertise. Bob Alward, Assistant Superintendent at the JDC, made several important 11th hour suggestions on the final draft. And Angie Johnson, beloved art teacher at the JDC, shared insights about residents and the need for art and self-expression during detention.

The Honorable Ed Post provided guidance regarding legal system issues for juveniles. I am grateful for his generous contribution to the novel's accuracy.

My dear friend, Nancy Jo Graham, shared poignant stories about her own journey as a clairvoyant child with artistic abilities. She responded to the novel-in-progress with special awareness and compassion for the character of Renata.

Thanks also to Sarah Mienel for insights into our local domestic crisis center operation. Thanks to readers Thea and Howard Datema and Kelly Oom. Thanks to RV Henretty-Jornales for his candor and integrity.

I am grateful for expert editing from Andrew Karre.

about the author

Margaret Willey has written numerous books for readers of all ages during a career that spans decades. She is the recipient of the Charlotte Zolotow Award, and her novels have been recognized by the ALA for excellence. She received the 2011 Gwen Frostic Award from the Michigan Reading Association, an award for impacting literacy in her state. She lives in Michigan with her husband. Visit her online at www.margaretwilley.com.